OF CRITTERS THAT GNAW OUR BONES

B.A.D.

As in order of…

A GIFT FROM IT

Otis pushed up on his tippy toes and reached high for the door knob. He extended his arm to its maximum limits, managing to get his fingers just barely around the cold nickel knob. Utilizing his monkey-like grip, Otis successfully achieved a twist as he pulled down, causing the large red door to swing open.

Immediately a rush of fall wind threw itself at him, overwhelming his senses with the warm autumn scent of burning wood and decaying leaves. He took a step forward out onto the porch and overlooked the early rumble of Halloween.

From his eyes, the world appeared to be glowing in amber, with the sun making its first contact with the horizon in descent, the

Jack O' Lanterns flickering their smiles as they lined up the front porches of the neighborhood, the yellow-orange leaves raining down from the trees that arched over the road, and the age-old street lamps warming up their lights after awakening from their internal clocks.

Otis observed the handful of crowds that had already begun their journey of visiting house to house; the adults standing at the edge of the sidewalks in their winter jackets, holding cups of coffee while watching their children sprint up and down the pathways, knocking on doors for candy.

All the children outside seemed to be dressed up in some form of modern-day Halloween apparel, such as the Transformers' characters, Pixar's most recent princess or hero, the latest video game's protagonist, or an outfit from the common section of Target's holiday display.

But Otis, naturally, was different. And though only the young age of six, he had always preferred the "classics" so to say. He favored the deep, true nature of holidays, and sought the family in Christmas, the life in Easter, the freedom in Summer, and the somber in Halloween.

His costume for this fine evening, was a handmade, hand-stitched Scarecrow suit, constructed of a rough wool for a vest with splintering straws of hay for details. It was an ugly sight, and yet this visual imperfection somehow made it all the more convincing.

Otis' mother made this costume for him... but she was not there to see him in it now.

He had learned over the years that when the dinning room table was flooded with dark green bottles alongside the funny shaped glasses that were wide at the top but skinny at the bottom, mother had gone to sleep in her bed. Otis once tried the strange, burgundy liquid long ago, when he stumbled upon a glass of it shattered on the ground. He smushed his finger into a pool of its watery substance, and brought the glossy glaze up to his lips, his face puckering upon contact as the contents were too bitter for his immature palate.

Usually, Otis would wait patiently for his mother to wake up when she entered this state of rest, but tonight, on this lonely festive gloam of Halloween, Otis' favorite holiday, he couldn't bear the stagnate passing of time. He worried that all the other houses might run out of candy by the time she awoke, or that she might acquire too strong of a migraine to take him out later as she always did and said, or maybe, just maybe, she would sleep the whole night through until morning.

Surely a child could not bear such a thought nor fathom the danger in what their idea of a smart compromise would be, so of course, the naive Otis decided to head out onto the streets all by himself.

With his costume on and pillowcase in hand, Otis marched down the cobbled-stone path and onto the sidewalk, marking the beginning of his night crusade for the sugared sweets. Having grown accustomed to the usual route his mother would take him on when Trick-or-Treating, Otis took a right turn and waddled down the sidewalk towards his first stop.

It was intimidating at first, as all the other children and adults towered over him. Negligently, their clumsy bodies would bump into his or their feet would accidentally step on his toes.

At first, Otis was caught off guard by this little care demonstrated by the other children, but even more so by the little caution displayed by the adults, who under the title of "grown ups", should have had his best interests in mind.

After only a mere dozen steps into this excursion, Otis was ready to cry.

It was too strange, too overwhelming.

He felt completely vulnerable and utterly powerless, and this feeling produced a discomfort in him similar to that of being naked and disturbed. These strangers that surrounded him couldn't care less about his well being as they continued to trample over him, failing to help comfort or clothe his situation.

Soon, Otis' hands began to blossom pearly sanguine beads of blood, a result of his palms scraping against the pavement from repetitively catching himself whenever knocked down. And his toes had also begun to swell plump n' purple, throbbing with penetrating aches upon each step taken from the constant stomping of feet by the neglectful walkers.

Interestingly enough, however, an oddity arose out of these mistreatments Otis endured, something that he took notice to right away; His balance had slowly become more sturdy and would remain unbroken during the bustle and pushes from greedy kids and ignorant elders. The pain that once took refuge in his feet and toes now idly began to fade away, replacing itself with a strange numbness that tingled in a buzzing-like, beehive manner. And the very essence that made up the foundation of Otis' feelings and emotions began to evolve into something else entirely.

He gradually started to understand the harsh truth that the people around him… didn't care of his presence.

He realized he was irrelevant to them.

His health, his emotional capacity, his happiness and safety— all meaningless. His purpose, though subjective to himself, was valueless to these zombie folk who strutted about.

Otis now understood that it was by his own care for himself that he would have to keep moving forward, and that there was no way else nor someone else who was going to get his bag filled with candy.

These people around him… they weren't going to disappear anytime soon, no matter how much he wished so.

And so, *strength* was the oddity that arose within him.

Otis trekked on and eventually reached a patch of dried roses and shrubbery that held still and lifeless, acting as a weird welcoming gate up the pathway to his first house-stop.

Otis felt his heart leap with excitement to the sight of the cobweb decor and the dormant plastic bats that hung from the roofing's drain pipe. He entered the property, crossing its front lawn before reaching the main porch, where he now stood bravely in front of its door. It was a mighty moment for him, as this slab of carved wood, pinned up and down with fake spiders, was now the only thing that remained between him and his reward. The candy within this house was only a mere action away, and so, Otis balled his hand into a fist.

He had never knocked on a door by himself before, since usually his mother would be the one to do that, leaving him with the simple task of saying "Trick or Treat!". But mother was not here this time, and the only thing that accompanied Otis on this solo journey was a pillowcase designated for the collecting of all his candy.

And so, with that knowledge, Otis raised his fist into the air cautiously, a build of intensity and anxiety behind it, and knocked.

Bup. Bup. Bup.

He collided the front of his four knuckles against the door, producing little noise. The wood was much denser and harder than he had expected, and caused a relative amount of offense in the joints between his fingers.

Otis decided to make a change in his method and adopted a different approach; he turned his wrist so his fist would face inward, and banged on the door once again but with the side of his hand this time.

Boom! Boom! Boom!

His forearms trembled from the recoil of vibration that rushed up his arm upon impact, and his ears jumped to the powerful bass it conjured.

A couple moments later and the door opened, revealing a young woman with an attractive face, dressed as a witch and holding a plastic cauldron that housed her supply of candy for the evening.

"Trick or Treat." said Otis in a voice just loud enough to reach the woman's ears.

"Ooo! A Scarecrow! I haven't seen a good costume like yours all night!" she pulled out a bite-size candy bar from her witch-bowl and dropped it in Otis' bag, "There yah are!"

Otis looked down into his bag, observing the fist token of his treasure hunt nestled all alone at the bottom, reflecting its cobalt-blue wrapper.

"Thank you!" he said before turning around and running his way back towards the street.

Upon reaching the sidewalk, a sense of satisfaction immediately engulfed Otis in a way which he had never felt before. He felt an air of pride in himself, one which gave birth to a courage he previously lacked, but would now accompany him on the way to his next house.

This new courage would only continue to grow and increase with each stop he made and the more candy that he piled up inside his bag.

Before Otis knew it, he had visited every house on the street and every house around the block in his neighborhood, his pillow sack now overbearingly heavy and almost half his own size. But the night was still young and the excitement from his independent successes made ending the hunt this early not such an easy task.

The bold young child looked past the houses at the end of the street and made a daring decision— he would go beyond the neighborhood.

With strides of confidence, his back hunched over to counter the immense weight of his candy bag thrown over his shoulder, Otis began the second half of his journey, bravely entering the unknown.

Gradually the streets lamps became more spaced apart, stretching further and further from each other, allowing more darkness to creep into the surroundings. But Otis was not scared by this added bleakness of the shadows, instead, he was quite the opposite and comforted by them.

Unlike most, Otis did not see the darkness as a camp for his enemies, but rather, a cloak for his own being. He felt hidden within the umbra, invisible almost. Concealment was now a given, and incognito the obvious.

But not all was black, at least not for long, as deeper into these strange lands Otis plunged, the more the trees became either scarce or empty of leaves. Only their twisted and accursed branches stretched grisly across the sky, and behind them a silver sliver of moonlight shinned through, piercing through the gaps and into Otis' dilated pupils.

This new shade of lighting manipulated the world around him into a different ambiance than the one back in his old neighborhood. Here, things seemed wicked, and the sound of his footsteps alone were a violation against its default state of silence.

Porch lights weren't on, the streets were empty, the wind didn't blow but howled, the nocturnal animals sang their midnight cries, and the air was just cold enough to dry the nostrils but not cold enough to dry the eyes.

You would think such a setting would be unsettling to a child and evoke some manner of terror, but as expected in the case of Otis— it did not. He was intrigued by this difference of night, as it felt truer to its own nature here than the false embodiment of it he was used to back home.

An hour had passed as Otis treaded deeper into this foreign terrain, with still no life in sight. He had almost forgotten the fact that he was searching for more houses in desire of candy, too absorbed in this mysterious new atmosphere, that is... until he stumbled upon a skinny light creeping its glow from out a tiny home.

Neurons fired off within Otis' hippocampus in a web-like flurry, as the sight of the house sparked a memory.

He recognized this house. In fact, he had been driven passed it many of times when his mother picked him up from Kindergarten.

It looked a lot different at night compared to its state during the day which he was more accustomed to seeing it in.

Usually, it appeared as a small, mint green house with a chestnut door and mocha roofing. A thin black gate bordered around its front yard, protecting the rich green grass and ceramic lawn decors within, while three porch steps lead to the large patio of the raised house. There, an old man usually sat on a rocking chair, observing the world passing him by from the single point of perspective. He had large glasses that made his eyes bigger than his face, shiny gray hair styled in a combover, and usually wore an attire involving the repetitive colors of peach and khaki.

Sometimes their eyes would meet, a quick ten second span during the car's passing, and during that fleeting moment, the old man would smile or sometimes even wave at Otis.

He seemed welcoming, approachable… and now it was his very house that held the only light amongst the black solitude of the street.

This light, Otis noticed, came not from a bulb above the doorbell nor the path-lights leading up to the porch, but rather through the narrow crack of the front door, just barely open an inch wide.

Otis approached the black iron gate and gave it a gentle push. A hollow screech echoed from its hinge's rotation while he continued to walk down the property's slim stone path towards the porch, his knees rising to his chest in order to climb their steep steps.

When Otis reached the door, he attempted his signature knock that had been getting a response from the other side all night long, only this time, after the first "Bang!" of contact, the door creaked open.

The light that had initially caught his attention became more visible with the larger opening of the door, shining blatantly from a specific room across the hallway that Otis was now looking down. The rest of the house was uncannily dark— pitch black and slurring with shadows in every space, nook and cranny… so it was only obvious that Otis would head towards the light.

The closer he drew near that room, the more he noticed a bizarre scent lofting about the air; meaty, but not of any carnivorous variation he had ever encountered. It was too foreign, and therefore, couldn't engage his appetite.

Once Otis reached the end of the hallway, the scent had become almost overwhelming, but with nowhere else to go and curiosity blooming in the child's mind, he promptly entered the room from which the light was emitting from.

And thats when he saw it, the source of illumination; an ancient looking lantern that encased the glow of a unique, silver color which Otis had never seen before. And even more peculiar than that, was the odd figure who's lap the lantern rest on.

Otis averted his eyes from the lantern to better observe the strange being who caressed the encasement of the light.

Sitting on the kitchen's marble counter top was a charcoal skinned creature with long pointed ears, a crude face, full black eyes lacking any white sclera, and a tiny body who's legs dangled off the edge of the counter, swinging back and forth.

This unnerving creature must have noticed Otis in its peripheral vision, as it slowly moved its eyes, followed by a turn of its head, until Otis was completely in its line of sight, observing the young child with a blithe curiosity.

Otis felt obligated to say something as the creature did not move, speak, nor even blink.

"Hi." said Otis, with the naivety only capable of a child.

The creature took one last look of Otis, up and down, before insouciantly responding, "Hello."

"What are you?" asked Otis.

"*It* is a Goblin, tiny human. What is *He* doing here?"

Otis looked over his shoulder and around the room, confused as to who the Goblin was addressing. "Who are you talking to?" he asked.

The Goblin simply lifted an arm off the lantern and pointed its finger at Otis.

"But, then who is He?" asked Otis.

The Goblin remained pointing at Otis.

It took Otis a few seconds for him to wrap his head around the strange grammatical structure of the Goblin's speech, but he quickly picked up on it; The Goblin referred to itself as *It*, and to Otis as *He*.

"Oh, I'm here for candy." answered Otis, proudly lifting up his impressively stuffed pillowcase for reference, "What are you doing here?"

The Goblin glanced over to the oven where digital numbers counted down and a small orange glow heated the contents within. "Making cookies" said the Goblin.

"Cookies!… They don't smell like normal cookies. Can I have one?" asked Otis.

The Goblin shook its head no, "They're Its special cookies. He would not like them, He should not eat of such fruits…not yet, at least."

"Well what's your name?"

The Goblin shifted uncomfortably from the question, "Humans are not to know of Goblins, but He is a tiny human and no threat to It, therefore, He should only refer to thee as It. 'Tis better that way."

"Okay" agreed Otis, absent of any fuss towards the request, "Are you friends with the old man that lives here?"

The Goblin huffed in a shallow laugh that gradually grew into a wild hysteria. "It would **never** be friends with such a beast! It came here *for* Him, not to *meet* Him."

"Oh. I sort of know him. When my mom picks me up from school, we drive down this street and sometimes I see him on the porch. Sometimes he waves to me."

The corners of the Goblin's mouth turned sour to Otis' words. "Yes. Him wreaked strongly this night. 'Tis how It found Him. Little humans like He's-self travel 'bout to many houses on All Hallows Eve. This gives beasts such as Him plenty to feast upon. He is lucky It smelled Him's evil before He arrived here, Him would have definitely taken He into Him's arms for indulgence should Him not be baking in the oven now."

Otis understood little of what the Goblin said. It didn't make any sense to him and the way the Goblin spoke didn't help his comprehension of the words either.

"You can smell evil?" asked Otis, "What does evil smell like?"

The Goblin shrugged, "Rancid like acid, metallic like coins, stale like mold, putrid like cheese— depends on the type of evil.

In the case of Him, Him smelt like rot and tooth decay. Most of the evil that preys on the purity of tiny humans smell as such.

It enjoys hunting such abominations like Him over all the other evils It encounters."

"Hunting?" questioned Otis, beginning to make sense of what might have happened now, recalling his school mate, Robby, speaking about his father who hunted animals, killing them in the process, "So did you…?"

The Goblin gave a single nod.

"And now he's…"

The Goblin nodded once again.

Otis pondered this news for a moment. His mother had told him that killing was wrong and that murderers would go to hell, and yet he couldn't help but feel safe in the presence of this Goblin. He didn't feel threatened nor in danger by the creature in any way.

"Killing is bad" began Otis, "And if you killed Him, then that must mean you're evil too… So what do you smell like?"

The Goblin's eyes lit up to the question, bringing on a sense of life that had not been there during It's previous, mundane engagement with Otis.

"Ahh, tiny human is wise. Tell It, what does He think It smells like?"

Otis shrugged, "I don't know."

"Take a guess. Does He think It smells like the other evils?"

Otis shook his head no.

"No?" the Goblin now shuffled on the counter, readjusting its position to fully face Otis' direction, "What does He think It smells like, then?"

Otis began drawing air into his nostrils in an attempt to pull a scent from the Goblin, but alas, he could not smell the evil.

"Different" answered Otis in his best guess.

The Goblin smiled, revealing its thin, sharp and surprisingly white, pointed teeth.

"He is correct! It is a different kind of evil!"

Otis scratched the back of his head, his costume having caused an itch to his scalp, "Were you always evil?" he asked.

"Not always" replied the Goblin, shaking its head. "It was once like tiny human. It couldn't smell evil, It wasn't evil, It was good. But after many realizations — dips into the hot pond, waters black of boiling mud — It came to many understandings about the world.

Life and death, the powers caught between them; good and evil.

And it was then that It finally understood that evil does not fear good, evil fears *greater* evil. And so It became that— the evil which evil fears, the evil the good prays for, the evil that darkness whispers about."

The Goblin then stuck out its long tongue and let it droop down beneath its chin, slithering and salivating. A strange sound resonated from deep within Its throat while producing a smile, eyes shut in pure bliss, "And It couldn't enjoy this anymore!"

Otis raised his hand and pointed to the lantern, "...And why do you carry that around?"

The Goblin squinted its eyes in fascination with Otis, its interest in the young boy only growing, "The lantern? Are you drawn by its light?"

Otis nodded, "It's pretty."

The Goblin smiled, "That it is. This lantern is Its purpose. The light within the dark, light that can only emerge when in the dark. Should the lantern be set in the sun, its glow shall never be seen, always hidden, never recognized. The light can only be noticed when submerged in black, the depths of evil, and scurry do the shadows run from its piercing rays. True potential only reached when plunged into hell."

Otis gnawed on his bottom lip with eagerness, wanting to hold the lantern but not wanting to ask for it, afraid that such a question would break manners and spoil his relationship with the Goblin— a result of strict parenting and all his misdoings (even be it minor) being met with unnecessary escalation.

"Is it heavy?" asked Otis.

The Goblin broke into laughter, throwing its head back and howling up towards the moon. "Does He wish to hold my lantern? Does He want it as his own?"... Suddenly the Goblin's smile dropped and its eyelids opened wider. Its face turned serious but in a positive manner, "Does He wish to be like It one day?"

The Goblin hopped off the counter, landing on its feet and slowly approaching Otis. "Three eyes open. Uncompromisable to anything but truth. Evil within thy own right. A beacon for the good who have been hurt by the bad."

The Goblin stopped a foot in front of Otis, coming face to face as they were both the same height.

Otis stared at the lantern in Its hands, wondering if the Goblin was going to hand it over to him.

"Sadly, It cannot give the tiny human Its lantern. However, 'tis All Hallows Eve, and should He say the right words, It can give He a treat…"

A silent pause filled their space until at last Otis caught on to what was being asked of him.

"Trick Or Treat!" said Otis, opening up his pillowcase with glee, "I can't take much more candy though. My bag's already heavy and I have to walk all the way back home with it."

"Do not worry, tiny human. What It is about to give He weighs nothing."

The Goblin snatched a piece of the air surrounding them with utter quickness, as if catching an invisible fly. It then moved its clenched fist over Otis' candy sack and opened, wiggling its fingers to ensure all of the invisible air fell in.

Otis looked down into the bag after the Goblin's little performance, expecting something to manifest itself in his candy sack. "What is it?" asked Otis, his tone more confused than disappointed.

The Goblin met its eyes with Otis'.

"Time." It said.

"He can't see it, it's invisible. He can't feel it, it weighs nothing. He can't hear it, it is silent. And He can't smell it, for it bears no scent. But make no mistake, it is the most powerful gift receivable.

With time, He will grow, and with growth comes maturity, understanding, realizations, and a change of self that He will be able to guide in any direction. Without a doubt, evil will invade He's life at some point, and it shall never truly leave after. When this happens, He will have many choices for going about it, and should He wish to be like It, He can wield a lantern of He's own making."

Otis squinted, frowned, and cocked his head, trying to make sense of what the Goblin had just said.

Beep! Beep! Beep! Beep!

A shrill sound rang four times, startling Otis and making him jump in place. The Goblin stayed steady however, impervious to the sound as if it had seen and known greater horrors that made its nerves immune to such trivial surprises.

The Goblin looked over its shoulder and towards the oven. "Its cookies are done." It then looked back at Otis, "And so is the conversation with tiny human. It smells no more evil lingering outside tonight. He should be safe on the journey back home."

The Goblin turned away and headed for the oven, but before Otis left, he asked the creature one more question, "Will I ever see you again?"

The Goblin stopped in its tracks but did not turn around, "Perhaps, 'tis possible, yes. But as It said before, Humans aren't to know of Goblins… but He is certainly different, so only time will tell." It put on a pair of mitts and opened the oven, "Goodbye, tiny human."

Otis watched the Goblin take a metal sheet out of the oven with awkward looking cookies sizzling on top from the exposure to cool air, before finally exiting the room and then the house altogether.

He trotted around the black fence and headed back down the street, this time walking in the middle of the road rather than on the sidewalk. It felt more immersive this way, like the trees were bowing before him in their crippling curves, and the moon's light was revealing a clairvoyant path before him. Like the flapping of bats' wings were actually applauding his walk, and the howling winds were, instead, cheers in his a favor.

Though he wasn't there yet, in this setting, Otis felt already at home.

Like clockwork, it took Otis another full hour to return to his neighborhood, eventually finding himself before the front door of his beloved house.

He reached up to turn the door handle, and found it surprisingly easier this time around than last he remembered when leaving the place.

He entered the dwelling, locked the door behind him, and headed towards the living room. As he passed the stairs which lead to the bedrooms, he could hear the faint sound of snores coming from his mother's room. She had slept the entire time Otis was away.

Otis continued on and then plopped down in the center of the living room's carpet, without even turning on the TV.

He opened up his pillowcase and peeked in to see the mountain of multicolor wrapped sweets heaping within.

During this spreading open of the bag, however, Otis was filled with a strange sensation. He didn't know what it was nor how to describe it, but it definitely stirred within his body and the networks of his mind.

A clarity overwhelmed him, and in this moment, he questioned the reality of the events which had just occurred that night. It was hard for him to wrap his head around it all, and he still didn't fully understand the meaning or the content behind the words spoken.

But in this moment, it did not matter, and Otis brushed aside this brief interruption, returning to his gleeful skimming of assorted candy in his collection. For one day, he would be able to make sense of all this, as the future held nothing ahead of him but time.

THE MAN WITH TWENTY FINGERS

The traditional book, quite often, will start its narrative with a description, an action, a setup, or even a modest message.

However, I find myself in the unique predisposition of offering an apology before my tale.

So I am sorry, Dear Reader, for this story is a strange one.

For preface, it was plucked from the enigmatic catacombs that contain all of our troubles. You know, that benighted place hidden deep within all us bipedal creatures. Only, this particular narrative of verity is in unusual contrast to the rest in its class.

I could go on to explain how, but I'd rather tell you the story first, and see if you come to the same conclusion on your own. So please, listen to my tale with astute discernment, and then after, tell me yourself about the Man with Twenty Fingers.

This all takes place in a world very similar to ours, only a bit more…odd.

In this world the flowers could sing, they had the most beautiful voices that thrilled their perceivers, and brought tears to all the orphans. For this reason, adults would often gather in the meadows, adorned in black tie and equipped with glasses of champagne. Here, they'd listen to the a cappella of sunflowers and the operas of echinaceas.

If you gave water sugar, it would grow two legs. If you gave it more sugar, it would begin to dance. Too often did kids play with their water, and in proper response, were constantly scolded.

Balloons were made of clay and painted by the parents. Should they ever let them go, well, they'd never float back down.

All businessmen were wolves, and they wore clown shoes. All politicians were clowns, and they wore brogues.

Everyone loved their Aunt Samantha, although Aunt Samantha didn't love everyone.

Everything living spoke the same language, yet still, some couldn't for the life of them hear the other.

But the strangest thing about this world, for some inescapable reason, was that its residents could only speak in rhyme.

You see, Dear Reader? It is just as I said, this world is very similar to ours, only more odd.

Now within this bizarre world stood a tiny hospital off the bank of a noisy interstate. It was surrounded by a countering silence of dense, redwood trees, creating a thick city of green that dampened the racket of passing cars.

Grey clouds of charcoal tone hung heavy above this building, though its gloom was constantly debated over being a product of the weather, or a result from the melancholy occupants inside.

Some cars would pull off of the freeway and enter the hospital grounds, while others left it, heading back onto the road with engines still cold.

This in-and-out flow was the main contributor to the small remnants of vitality that existed within this desolate place; like the circulation of blood throughout the body, though no one would consider the hospital to be its heart.

On the fourth floor of the establishment, lit only by naked florescent lights and littered with distant wails, lied a young, pretty woman. She was particularly skinny, arousing a discomfort to the sight of the large bump that protruded from her belly in abnormal contrast to her small frame.

She had just begun labor and her screams were quickly followed by a group of doctors who now assembled in her room, causing the already tiny space between the walls to feel even tinier.

The young woman in labor could not tell if these people who now shared the room with her were truly doctors, or perhaps empaths, or possibly deceptive lyrebirds, as they all seemed to mock her in some fashion. When she cried, they panicked. When she screamed in pain, they winced and flinched. When she begged with questions, they questioned her back with similar topics. And whenever she pushed, they instructed her to push more.

Distinguishing their true identity felt too hard a task, and with the young woman in labor's energy rapidly dropping, she decided to put all her focus on pushing the baby out.

There was for an instant, a singular, still, and fleeting moment of absolute silence, for once the young mother was no longer in labor and ceased her wails, the screams were immediately replaced by the new form of life that had just escaped the cavity of her flesh.

The offensive sound of scissors snapped and the doctors began to inspect the baby, for an alarming notice was discovered almost immediately— the baby boy had twenty fingers.

One Doctor said, "This boy is very different."
While another Doctor said, "This boy is very special."
A third Doctor said, "This boy must be a miscreant."
While the fourth Doctor said, "He could never be
Aunt Samantha's vessel."

With a hesitance that appeared to be of their own interest and volition, the doctors slowly handed the baby boy with twenty fingers to his mother, wrapped in a pale blue cloth with blood still smeared on his brow.

The young mother smiled at the sight of her child and coddled his face gently with her first two fingers.

The doctors all gave passing glances to each other before continuing their rant to what they now thought was a *delusional* young mother.

"The boy is a monster," said the nearest doctor.
"You can put him in foster," said the furthest doctor.
"This boy's existence is foul!" Said the most hateful doctor.
But the mother shut them all down when she proclaimed,
"This boy is Reed Doyar Raue."

He now had a name, and more importantly, a loving mother…but sadly, neither one those gifts would stick around for long.

With a birth certificate signed and forty eight hours having passed, the baby boy with twenty fingers — named Reed Doyar Raue — left the hospital with his mother, just as a blaring orange sun broke through those dark clouds that so dutifully floated above the bleak building.

Life would seem pleasant for that newborn baby when turning his eyes to the future, however as we all know, life is never so easy.

All that love, care, gentleness, soothing words, selfless patience, and unconditional acceptance would disappear along with the mother when she passed away at his tender age of five.

His name, like the infant duckling in short dawdle from the mama duck's tail, would shortly follow her lead. Peers and adults alike had ceased to call him by the words his mother announced at his birth, "Reed Doyar Raue", and instead began to refer to him as *The Boy with Twenty Fingers.*

He was all alone. Without a mother, without peers, without a family, without friends. Without anyone who looked like him, anyone who could relate to him, anyone who could like him, and so The Boy with Twenty Fingers wished only that he could be normal.

So it was that the wish to be normal would never seem to leave him, not during his estrangement through childhood, or his excision through adolescence.

Perhaps if his mother had lived, the young boy would come to know stoicism. Maybe the mantle of an outcast would ricochet off his shoulders by the countless lessons, drilling of self love, and tough skin the mother would have instilled in him.

But alas, she had not lived, and such teachings of life never managed to reach the young, pitiful child.

By natural order of fleeting time, The Boy with Twenty Fingers soon came to be called *The Man with Twenty Fingers.*

Donning a new maturity with age, the Man with Twenty Fingers no longer wished he could be normal, for he was far too wise for such a thing. He knew such a wish was too far out of grasp. So he changed it. Changed it to something more reasonable in manner, one that no longer made him a fool, nor carried the ignorance of youth. He had found something more attainable in his adulthood, and that was to *dream* he was normal. And this would come to be all he ever dreamed of.

But what kind of story would this be if it didn't have a turn of events?

For exactly that happened, a turn of events so to say, one that not even The Man with Twenty Fingers could've expected nor achieved in his wildest of dreams.

The mailman dropped off his post in the usual, timely fashion— 10 a.m. on the dot to be exact, beckoning the Man with

Twenty Fingers' retrieval with the brass clanking of the mail slot's lid, like a hungry pet to the feeding bell.

Amongst his common papers sat a quaint yellow envelope, discolored but not ragged, that managed to catch his attention. There was no return address nor even his own, simply his birth name written in beautiful calligraphy on the back.

"Reed Doyar Raue," he said aloud.

The Man with Twenty Fingers felt as though he had nearly forgotten that was his name, and felt a warm sensation to be addressed by it again despite not knowing who, what, or where it was from.

He flipped over the envelope to be met with yet another alluring mystery to intrigue his psyche; a wax seal bearing the image of an unlit candle, keeping its contents shut.

The symbol rang no bells to the Man with Twenty Fingers, but the whole surprise and endearment upon hearing his birth name once again brought on a fond nostalgia, the likes of which he had only experienced when his mother was still alive.

With extreme caution, the Man with Twenty Fingers delicately opened the letter, ensuring both the wax seal and calligraphic envelope remained fully intact with no defacement.

Inside was a three fold letter, written in the same dark ink with the same handwriting as his name on the envelope.

It read,

"The answer you've been looking for is at W Hier Yionae Tudare Dr.
But there's a strict condition required to arrive.
You cannot drive, you cannot sail, you cannot bus, you cannot fly.
This journey must be made on foot, without exception, you must comply.
You may eat when you're hungry, from a restaurant or from trash.
Doesn't matter if you steal it, or pay for it in cash.
You may sleep when you're tired, in bedding or the ground.

You may disclose your journey's secret, or never make a sound.
It matters not what you do, how you do it, or do it with.
Just as long as you walk, the destination will hold your gift."

The Man with Twenty Fingers had never felt something like this before. The emotion was beyond hope, for this mysterious letter was a *guarantee*. Should he smile, cry, squeal, or sing and dance? How would one encapsulate such a surge of energy upon receiving such a blatant answer to life?

To his surprise, the Man with Twenty Fingers found his response in his upstairs closet, as his response was action.

"For reasons unknown even to I," he said aloud,
"I will wear my red velvet lapel tux, with a purple tie!"

He dressed as quick as he could while ensuring to not fault the elegance essential to the tux's tedious precision, then ran straight out of the door.

At first he sprinted down the streets and the surrounding neighborhood homes, but his joints began to creak and his thighs were quick to burn from such an alacritous venture. So, The Man with Twenty Fingers slowed his speed to a jog where he found himself able to catch his breath and pace his movements, but even that didn't last for too long.

In time he adopted to skipping, bounding down the blocks until his feet grew sore, while swinging his arms for momentum and waving to pedestrians in ecstasy.

That, too, went on for some distance until The Man with Twenty Fingers found himself forced to settle with walking, having realized that he was only twenty blocks away from his home while the destination holding his answer was still a staggering trek's journey away.

The letter was correct, this was indeed a journey. So he came to terms with the walk and relinquished his impatience, moving forward without any of the rush and embracing the time-teased flow that impregnates any travel.

The destination was not fleeting nor limited by time, so the Man with Twenty Fingers strode confidently in observation, enjoying the passing of surroundings as he made his way to his answer.

He was still just steps into his long travel when a sweet, yet juicy scent riddled with spices of licorice, fennel, and garlic caught his attention with its smokey contents drifting into his nose.

This made The Man with Twenty Fingers hungry, so he followed the smell that lofted an invisible path in the air to a butcher's shop nearby.

The bell rang joyfully as he entered the establishment, and a heavy but hearty looking man approached the counter to serve him.

"Hello there, dear fellow.
I am the Butcher who sells sausage.
Do you prefer spicy, smokey, sweet, mellow?
There's beef, horse, pork, lamb and ostrich."

The Man with Twenty Fingers smiled as his stomach growled in anticipation.

"I'll take all four flavors, two of each please.
How much do you charge for this little feast?"

The Butcher dropped his head with a somber expression to The Man with Twenty Finger's order, and replied in a disheartened voice,

"I'm so sorry to say, my good dear fellow,
That I can only give you one of the spicy, smokey,
sweet, and mellow."
"Do not worry, my good Butcher, I'll gladly take the four.
But why ever could a Butcher not produce more?"

Asked the Man with Twenty Fingers.

"Well, I once had a rod, about a finger in size.
And when I filled my sausages, I'd watch how they rise.
When the casing was filled to the size of the rod,
I'd stop and start the next, stacking identically sized pods.
But one day I lost it, never again to be found.
And since then, no sausage of mine is perfectly
shaped when bound.
I've wasted so much meat from the constant disproportions,
That my banking and my repute have both received demotions.
No longer can I buy in bulk nor even discard scraps.
I must buy all my meat frugally then force it all in wraps."

The Man with Twenty Fingers pitied the Butcher and wished so strongly to help, so much so that a bright idea managed to cross his mind.

"My dear good Butcher, if I may,
I'd like to give you more than money as a form of pay.
Upon my hands you'll come to see,
I have twenty fingers, ten too many.
If you'd like, you can have one, as I've come to believe,
That with it, your answer just might be achieved."

The Butcher looked up from the soft mount of neck fat that supported his fallen head, while his sorrowful eyes now took sight of the fingers belonging to the generous customer before him. And to his amazement and ultimate glee, one finger did hold the same dimensions as the small rod he once used to measure all his sausages!

And so The Many with Twenty Fingers parted with one of his extra fingers, along with most of the money on his person, while taking his four sausages, one spicy, one smokey, one sweet, and one mellow, and continued his journey to the mysteries address.

The Butcher, ever grateful, ever thankful, and ever appreciative, returned to making identical sized sausages of equal portions, buying meat in bulk and discarding the scraps.

The Man with Twenty Fingers went on to eat his sausages as he continued to walk down the street. At first he felt the satisfaction of his hunger beginning to fade, but noted a new feeling that seemed to blossom and now lingered, one unrelated to the sausages he consumed.

That feeling was fulfilling itself, a fulfilled feeling from a source more centered to that of his chest as opposed to his stomach.

> "For what reason does my chest feel packed?
> Like the warmth of the sun was folded and stacked,
> Shoved into my heart behind the rib-bones' rack,
> When the sausage can only enter my stomach track?"

Asked The man with Twenty Fingers to himself.

> "I feel so happy, no, I feel good,
> All 'cause I helped the Butcher like one should,
> Or perhaps 'cause I helped the Butcher because I could,
> Or perhaps 'cause if roles were reversed- I'd appreciate
> such help, or rather, I know I would."

Having been different, special, an outcast, unfitting, a monster, unwanted, and foul all his life, The Man with Twenty Fingers had never found himself on the opposing side of meeting someone else in need of an extra hand. This was in fact the first time he had encountered such a situation, and he never knew that *being* the person who he had always prayed would come to *his* rescue would ever feel so good.

He even debated in this moment the idea of who had it better; was it the feeling the recipient attained, or the feeling the giver gained?

From that moment on, the Man with Twenty Fingers vowed he would help every single soul in need whose path he crossed along his quest to the mysterious location!

And it would just so happen that another calling was only a foot away…

His nose tingled once more to a tantalizing scent, not enamored by food but rather bewitched like dreams.

He stopped in his tracks and turned to see what little shop had this time aroused his being.

It was a florist shop. Tiny, but beautiful, even magical some would say, with vines cascading in a fruitless climb alongside the top of building's brick exterior, while green extravagance decorated the large crystal windows that displayed an array of magnificent flowers fit for a royal wedding on the inside. Various pots coddled a multitude of flora, swaying delicately with the wind as they hung from the awning that protruded over the entry.

Being adorned in a tux with no flower in its pocket, and tempted by the glamour of the delightful scent, The Man with Twenty Fingers decided to enter the little green shop.

As soon as he entered through its doors, fresh, bright air, crisper than that of an ocean front, swept over his face and into his lungs, and a grin appeared across his face before the dopamine had even the slightest chance of saturating his brain.

"Good day, dear fellow,
Fancy a flower for a date?
We have pink, red, blue, and yellow,
Why leave love to the hands of fate?"

Said the golden haired Florist who owned the shop.

"Good day, my dear lady.
Not a date but for my tux.

Perhaps a white flower would pair most greatly,
For the death of my past at this journey's end, with any luck."

"I have just the right blossom, I use them myself,
For the death of my business and the death of my wealth."

Said the Florist dolefully.

"Tell me, dear Florist, what has you so glum?
I just helped another solve his own conundrum."

"These flowers, right here, I've failed them so.
Their stalks keep collapsing, pointing once at heaven,
but now toes.
I've given them water, extra sun, and even prayed,
But without a proper stake, tall they've never stayed."

The Man with Twenty Fingers observed the flowers at hand. There were three lilies in a small clay pot of soil to which he took notice of, with their pitiful orange petals slumped heavily in their own dirt.

He lifted one up, straightening it to stand, but as soon as he let go it collapsed once again. A stake was indeed needed for such a plant, but the Man with Twenty Fingers did not have such a tool on him.

But then it struck his mind like a bolt of lightning or a blacksmith's hammer, as another idea appeared that could aid this person in need.

He proceeded to break off another one of his extra fingers and handed it to the Florist.

"Take this, my dear lady, an extra finger of mine,
And use it as a stake for the flowers, becoming its new spine.
It seems to be the perfect height and the perfect size.
With this the flower can stand up straight, dismissing its need to die."

The Florist, ever grateful, ever thankful, ever appreciative, took the finger and tied it to the flowers' stem. After which she plucked the best white flower in her most beautiful collection and gave it to the Man with Twenty Fingers.

He said his goodbyes, gave his farewells, then stepped back out onto the street.

Ever so gently as to not disturb the soft petals, he tucked the white flower into the front chest pocket of his tuxedo and continued on his journey.

Countless more blocks were crossed and countless more miles he strode, and soon the fatigue that had silently pursued him had now caught up and set into his core.

It was getting dark outside, and the stars began to slowly take their place on the steel-blue blanket in their assigned order upon the sky, while The Man with Twenty Fingers, too, was forced to realize his assigned position of nighttime— the lying on his side and falling into dreams.

With this fact in mind, he made the decision to find the nearest Inn where he could rest through the dark and continue his existence in the morning.

Not too far, only three blocks more, was he able to stumble upon a three story house that featured his needs. Its lights were on, its gate was open, and the words "Bed 'n' Breakfast" stretched boldly across its door.

Relief caressed the Man with Twenty Fingers intimately, and he entered the well lit Inn.

Its structure was old, made by a generation past, but The Man with Twenty Fingers noticed that its paint was fresh and new.

It was painted all white, with different red decor covering the majority of its interior; the floor with carpets, the wall with paper, and windows with curtains. It was not unsightly, but rather a masked truth. This building that held the amenities of common life and simple needs was all too slanted. With its base and structure created of a time bygone, the newly fitted innards could not hide its faulty layout. No matter the paint, furniture, or decor, such a standing would never do in a living, but alas, one needs a place to sleep and eat lest they should survive night-fall.

The Man with Twenty Fingers made his way further in, discovering an older gentleman who stood behind a makeshift counter in what must have been the living room.

"Good evening, my fine gentleman, and how do you do?
This is my humble establishment, would you like a room?
The price is reasonable, but for you I'll cut a deal.
For a fellow gentleman like yourself, I'll give you a steal!"

The Man with Twenty Fingers knew he could use a discount for what little money he possessed, but while reaching for his pocket to reveal his wallet, he instantly remembered that he had no cash as it had all been spent at the Butcher's for the sausages he ate earlier.

"Good evening, dear Innkeeper, but I'm sorry to say…
My pockets are empty, I have no means to pay.
I spent it on food, I'm on a journey you see,
But I have no expectation you'll let me stay for free.
Could we strike a deal though, an exchange or a trade?
I can give you one of my extra fingers, but that is all I'm afraid."

The Man with Twenty Fingers snapped off another one of his extra fingers and handed it to the Innkeeper, hoping such an offering would be sufficient.

The Old Innkeeper studied it intensively, rotating it slowly to inspect every detail that belonged to it.

"Okay," said the Innkeeper, "I'll make you this deal,
One night for one finger, that is your steal."

The Man with Twenty Fingers accepted the bargain with swiftness and thanked the Innkeeper before making his way up the stairs to the second floor, where he found his adequate allotted room and tucked away for the rest of the night.

His sleep was deep, sound, and rejuvenating— in his own words, it would have been labeled exquisite. But the Man with Twenty Fingers was not on an expedition of repose, but one of discovery; he was going to find the answer he had always been looking for, so sleep, though luxurious, was only temporary.

He awoke early in the morning, had a good stretch, put back on his tux, and left his room speedily, for today was the day that he would reach his destination.

Upon closing the door behind himself and locking it with the key, a hollow sound of banging captured the Man with Twenty Fingers' attention.

He trotted towards the source of the noise, entering the center of the stairway, but still did not see anything unusual that could have been its origin. But then it sounded again, that strange hollow banging, allowing him to finally pinpoint its direction.

The Man with Twenty Fingers ascended up the stairs, curious to uncover the explanation for this bizarreness.

While ascending from the second floor, on his way to what would have been the third, he came across a frustrated woman who was banging on a large slab of glass that blocked off the stairway from reaching the third and final floor.

Once again The Man with Twenty Fingers was puzzled by the quizzical architecture of this building, and approached the woman in his confusion.

> "Hello dear lady, I'm a previous resident of this Inn,
> Whatever is that piece of glass doing where the third floor
> begins?"

He asked.

"Hello dear fellow, I am a current resident of this here Inn,
As to this piece of glass you inquired about,
where ever do I begin.
My room is up there on the top third floor,
however I can no longer enter,
As the Innkeeper has installed this piece of glass
which blocks the stairway's center.
I've spoken to him and he will not remove it no matter what I say,
Tells me I'm in denial, I am angry for no reason,
I'm equal to all residents but still causing a fray.
He says the glass has always been there, always will be,
and it's better that way,
But my room is on that third floor, and this glass is
blocking where I've payed to stay."

The Man with Twenty Fingers felt revolted by the predicament that
the woman was in, and asked how he could help.

"Thank you dear fellow, I appreciate the gesture.
But the Innkeeper will not budge, no matter the pressure.
He told me the glass keeps the Inn proper,
its existence has no impurities,
But no matter how many finger prints I leave on it,
he seems blind to its new insecurities."

The Man with Twenty Fingers investigated the slab of glass, taking
note to all the finger prints the woman had smudged onto its surface.

"If he won't see yours, perhaps he'll see mine.
If he sees me as an equal, then my prints won't be so benign.
Take this extra finger and smudge out all of the shine,
Then the nasty Innkeeper will be forced to refine."

The Man with Twenty Fingers pulled off one of his extra fingers and handed it to the Inn's Resident. Ever grateful, ever thankful, ever appreciative, the woman took the finger and began to smear its print all over the glass slab.

As The Man with Twenty Fingers made his way downstairs, he passed a few words to the Innkeeper while walking out the door.

> "How horrid and dreadful this establishment must be,
> To allow such a dirty glass to block the third story.
> Go take a look for yourself, its sight is ungodly,
> I couldn't fathom to return, 'less its removal be
> handled promptly."

And with that, he tossed his room key to the Innkeeper and left, joyfully taking to the sidewalk and moving onwards toward his answer.

After many more miles but this time well paced, The Man with Twenty Fingers once again found himself encountering a strange noise that stole his attention. An abrupt and unpleasant cacophony of metal bangs and clangs shot sharply out of a nearby alley.

He decided to divert off path and take a peek down the mischievous alley, where more banging and clanging continued to erupt until his curiosity got the better of him and he waltzed down its cobbled path.

It was there where he found the source of all the racket; a cat jumping dumpster to dumpster, trash bin to trash bin, scattering about a whole mess of litter.

> "Excuse me, dear Cat, I don't mean to intrude,
> But what ever are you doing, if such a question isn't rude?"

The Cat stopped its rummaging and looked The Man with Twenty Fingers up and down.

"Hello there, dear human, I'm glad you asked!
I'm hungry—no—starving, and looking for scraps.
These humans must be fat as they leave no crumbs behind.
Would you happen to have any food? If not,
you're wasting my time."

The Man with Twenty Fingers felt bad for the cat as he, too, was once starving at the beginning of his journey — before he ate those sausages from the Butcher. But without a doubt, this Cat's predicament was worse. It was skinny, eyes sunken, tongue dry, hair falling, nutrients had not reached its body for weeks or months now.

"Unfortunately I do not have any food scraps or shavings,
But perhaps…just perhaps…I might satisfy your craving."

The Man with Twenty Fingers ripped off one of his extra fingers.

"Here, eat this, it's one of my extra fingers.
Take its nutrition and energy quickly, and do not linger.
For far back that way, the way I came,
You'll find a shop that sells meat with a butcher of large frame.
I just gave him a finger too, though it was for a different use,
But he now has plenty of scraps to fill you up from tail to tooth."

The Cat, ever grateful, ever thankful, ever appreciative, took The Man's finger and ate it. After which he pounced out of the trash bin and out into the street, making a dash for the butchery with the newfound energy it had just received.

And with that The Man with Twenty Fingers also left the alley, taking back to the sidewalk and his original path for his journey.

Not too far from the alley did the he begin to pass a cemetery, a boundless field gated up at the sidewalks edge. Beyond the metal rods breathed a land of different air from the street side view where

The Man with Twenty Fingers observed from. Vast and dark, a twilight frozen in time, familiar yet distant, a beautiful place indeed.

A figure then caught his eye in the near distance, something that looked like a standing shadow, or the Grim Reaper himself. But as The Man with Twenty Fingers got closer, he realized it was only the Groundskeeper dressed in a pitch black robe, frozen like a statue in his decrepit body, pointing down the street from where he had just came.

"…Are you alive, Dear Groundskeeper, if so I'd wish a good day.
But most of all I'd like to know why you point back that way?"

A slow and rough voice bellowed from the Groundskeeper, like stone rubbing against stone, startling The Man with Twenty Fingers into a gentle hop.

"Good day, Dear fellow, I assure you I'm alive.
You seem a bit shaken, I guess you found it a surprise.
Too often I see the living come here to cry tears all over their dead,
But the dead desire no pity, no, they desire flowers instead.
However, the living don't bring any, though I wish they would,
And so here at the gate I assume my duty and ever since have stood,
Pointing the way for all the living before they pass through,
To the direction of the florist shop, so they bring flowers
and not their blues."

The Man with Twenty Fingers smiled, as he already knew how he could help.

"Allow me, Dear Groundskeeper, to lend you a hand,
Or rather an extra finger, to free you from where you stand.
Take this here appendage and use it as best fit,
Whether it's tying it to the gate, or tying it to a stick.

But use it nonetheless, to point towards the florist in your place,
And return to the land of the dead, where your decrepitness
holds grace."

The Man with Twenty Fingers broke off one of his fingers and once again gifted it away. The Groundskeeper, ever grateful, ever thankful, ever appreciative, took the finger from The Man.

"Before you go, Dear Fellow, may I ask,
What brings you to the cemetery, if not for the dead,
then what task?"

"I am on my way to find my answer, it lies at
W Hier Yionae Tudare Dr.
I just happened to have passed you and lent a quick
hand before I could arrive."

"W Hier Yionae Tudare Dr.? Ah yes, I know of the place.
In fact you can be there in half the time, if you take the
shortcut and keep that same pace.
Straight through the cemetery, a direct cut across,
and you'll arrive on the other side.
It's a shortcut indeed, a much faster route,
it'll only take half the time."

The Man with Twenty Fingers was ecstatic at the news of this shortcut, and followed its path right away. He entered under the broad heavy gates of the cemetery and strode down the dry dirt road of the eerie graveled graveyard.

Pine tress cascaded along bumpy hills of fog-drowned tombstones, small hollow birds darted from bush to shrub with their agile flight, blackberries and thorns bloomed in a malevolent pattern amongst the deadman's land, and a peaceful but melancholy wind whistled a constant tune of alertness.

For most patrons of this cemetery, they would identify this gloom which breathed over the corpse filled acres to be omnipotent. However, the Man with Twenty Fingers couldn't feel more at home in this setting. Unbeknownst to him from infantile amnesia, but still carrying a torch in the deepest layer of his subconscious, this was the same atmosphere in which he was born; a familiar setting to that purgatory of a hospital where he suffered his birth into the world.

He smiled to the darting birds that passed his body by merely feet or inches. He plucked the berries from the bushes and suckled the juice from their pearly ripe clustered shells, then would prick his finger on a thorn from that same brush to return a drop of blood as repayment for his consumption. He listened to the wind's whistle and would occasionally whistle back to contribute to its conversation. And he would kick the pine cones in his path to help spread the seeds of the trees, so they may one day have children who grow up healthy.

But along this path in the cemetery, a new sound caught the ear of the Man with Twenty Fingers. The gentle sniffles, hiccups, and heaves of a secret cry, one which the bearer did not want anyone to hear.

The Man with Twenty Fingers followed the sound of these hushed wails until he found the source of this mourning.

A little girl, around the tender age of nine, was balled up — knees to chest — with her head hidden in her lap, crouched beneath one of the pine trees.

"Excuse me, young miss, do you happen to be lost?
You shouldn't be here alone so young,
no matter what pain may cost.
If you need to find the exit, I have no problem
guiding you back,
Just be sure to remember your way next time,
and never go off track."

"I'm not lost, mister, I'm hiding and I'm sad.
This is where my mother was buried, and I'm visiting with my dad.
Its been three years since my mother passed away,
And ever since then we visit her here on that day.
My father said he had a gift, a present from my mom.
He handed me her wedding ring as if my tears would calm.
But now my mourning's even worse and I can't see the
ring with glee.
For its fingerless image is just a reminder, and her bind
size is far too large for me."

The Man with Twenty Fingers shared the Girl's sadness, as he, too, carried a void of his mother's parting from his childhood. He wished he could hug the girl and take all her pain away, or tell her how with time it'll ease, but never fully fade. But he knew all the better, having been in her shoes before, so instead he decided to quell the agony that seized her in this moment now.

"Here, young miss, may this stop your tears?
If only temporarily, like a nightlight tempers fear.
It may not bring her back, and certainly won't fill your heart,
But at least you can look at the wedding ring, without
falling apart."

The Man with Twenty Fingers snapped off another one of his fingers, and gave it to the little Girl. She took the finger, ever grateful, ever thankful, ever appreciative, and hesitantly slid her mother's wedding ring on it, adopting a large smile when it stuck and didn't slide off.

"Oh it's perfect! The wedding ring fits!
I'm reminded of her when I see it now, and not the vacant bits!
Thank you so much, my appreciation is grand!
Now I must find my father, he must be a worried man."

"I'm glad you feel better, and I'm sorry for your loss.
I shall point your father in your direction, should our
paths cross."

And with that the Man with Twenty Fingers went on his merry way.

It wasn't too far from the location of the little girl that he began to hear another serving of sobs, perhaps a hundred feet or so from where he consoled the sad child.

But these cries were more hushed and intertwined with some words, too loud to be considered whispers, but definitely of quiet council.

The Man with Twenty Fingers followed the sound until he found who he assumed to be the father of the young girl, who was kneeling over a tombstone, speaking gently to its sacred space while watering its fresh flowers with his tears.

The Man with Twenty Fingers cautiously approached the man, hoping not to intrude, but enter respectfully into the man's domain of prayer.

"Excuse me, dear sir, I wish not to interrupt,
But I find myself with urgent knowledge which
I must pass on abrupt.
You're daughter is about ye that way, and is
searching for you now.
To let her be by herself any longer,
would make even the worst parent scowl."

The Mourning Husband brushed away his tears and looked at the Man with Twenty Fingers before rising to his feet.

"I apologize, good sir, I did not mean to lose her.
But when I gifted her the wedding ring,
it caused a bit of a stir.
She burst into tears then ran to the trees before
I could say a word,

And so I've been speaking to the grave of my wife,
hoping to be heard."

The Man with Twenty Fingers sought to ease the Mourning Husband's dread, so he informed him of his interactions with the little girl and how the daughter now bore a finger that could fit the mother's wedding ring, easing her momentary suffering…but such news only made the Mourning Husband cry more.

"Thank you, good sir, truly I appreciate it.
But the wedding ring and my daughter's tantrum is not the
reason for my own fit.
You see, I was recently in an accident,
one that caused me bodily harm.
I should count myself lucky for only losing a finger,
when I almost lost an arm.
But now when I hold my daughter's hand,
she can sense a piece of me is gone,
And I hurt at the thought that she now thinks
I'm next to be buried away in this lawn."

The Man with Twenty Fingers smiled with a warm heart, already aware to how he could help, and snapped off one of his extra fingers.

"Take this, dear sir, and wear it as your own.
Hold your daughter's hand in reassurance,
and consider your shame agone."

The Mourning Husband took the finger, ever grateful, ever thankful, ever appreciative, and put it on his hand. After which, he headed down the directed path and called for his daughter's return, soon leading to their reunion.

And with that, The Man with Twenty Fingers continued his journey with its end growing uncannily near, and a newfound set of nerves slowly setting into his stomach.

After having walked for thirty more minutes, The Man eventually came to notice a peculiar sight in the nearby distance.

Further ahead lie the opposite gate of the cemetery's encircling fence, signaling his achievement of arriving to the other side and a successful journey across the graveyard.

Beyond the heavy gate of the cemetery's end stood a tall hill that peaked straight into the sky. It did not touch the clouds, but did burn the eyes with how close it reached to the blazing rays of the sun. From that hill and all the way back down to the cemetery's gate, the sky was completely clear of the graveyard's hanging gray, and instead was replaced with a golden film of sunshine and nurtured greenery of grass and thriving life.

"This must be it!" thought the Man with Twenty Fingers as he continued on his way.

However, when he reached the edge of the cemetery and was creeping upon its gates, a shadowed flash caught his peripheral from within the last mausoleum that stood at the borders.

The Man With Twenty Fingers turned his gaze towards the deteriorating mausoleum to see whatever it could be that grabbed his attention in such an evasive sneak, and noticed two whites of eyes nearly hidden in the cascaded darkness from deep within that crypt.

The Man gave a friendly wave to the stranger lurking within, but was taken aback when those whites of the mysterious figure's eyes filled with fear and retreated immediately back into its shadows.

Having seen too much pain on this long path to find his answer, The Man with Twenty Fingers decided to investigate this fearful stranger further and see if he could possibly help them too.

The Man only made it three steps down before a a rough voice, burnt like charcoal, aged like dry lakes, and crumbled like limestone, hissed him away.

"Begone, human! And don't you come back!
I refuse to be victim of another attack!"

"I'm sorry, dear stranger, I mean you no harm.
I would never bestow you pain, I would only muster charm.
I was just heading to the hill that lies beyond the gates,
When I saw your fearful eyes, and thought that it could wait.
For what ever is the reason that you live in such fear,
And keep to shadows, casting me out of here?"

The fearful eyes that were only visible by their whites began to relax after hearing the words from The Man with Twenty Fingers, donning a rather tired look. From out of the shadows stepped a small creature, skinny with protruding bones, pale with visible veins, horns protruding from its skull and two tusks for bottom teeth.

"I am the Cryptid, and this is my home.
I keep my business to myself, and live a life alone.
I like this weather and prefer the dark, especially where it's cold,
But since I look like this and live here, I am a monster, at least
that's what you're told.
For so long now have humans put me down,
And even longer has their violence replaced their frowns.
Beaten, cursed, spat at, threatened, screamed at, chased with
torches, pitchforks and hooks.
And the worst part of it all is that one look was all it took."

The Man With Twenty Fingers felt his heart drop to his stomach and a nauseating sickness overfill his state of being. He, too, knew what it was like to be outcasted for nothing but one's own predetermined physical appearance, and empathized with the Cryptid.

"However can you make it stop, this evilness
from the human beings?
I will assist you however I can, for I, too,
know the pain from these things."

"There is no point, it cannot be stopped,
believe me I have tried.
'Tis why I hide in these shadows, safe in here,
and never peek outside.
The moment they see a glimpse of my form,
everything is set in stone,
And yet they are always the ones who creep in my shadows,
when I only wish to be left alone."

The Man with Twenty Fingers thought long and hard, burning
with a deep desire to free the Cryptid from this awful torment that
it had countlessly suffered time and time again. And so it was with
great glee that he delivered his idea to the Cyptid when the answer
crossed his mind.

"I have an idea, dear Cryptid, that I think might just work.
One where you may stay in your shadows and
ward off any who might lurk.
Take this, my extra finger, and use it as a ploy.
And then when the next human takes an interest,
you need no longer be coy.
Thrust it out of the shadows, so all they see is its point,
Then scream at them to leave at once,
and I promise it won't disappoint.
One look at the finger and they will think you are human,
An angry one, at that, with your voice of a demon.
Off they will go, running away in terror.
Making a confrontation with you… that much rarer."

With the Cryptid's agreement to his plan, The Man with Twenty Fingers ripped off his extra finger and gently placed it in the Cryptid's hand. Ever grateful, ever thankful, ever appreciative, the Cryptid walked The Man out of his mausoleum and returned that initial wave he was given earlier, waving him goodbye from the edge of the graveyard as The Man with Twenty Fingers hiked his way up to the top of the hill.

Embarking up the the mountain-like hill, the enlightening sun who's golden blaze engulfed all under its glare began to warm The Man's soul, recharge his cells, cleanse his palate, and rejuvenate his senses as he forged closer to its rays, nearing the top of its peak. From his newfound perspective of the mound's upper cap, a single tree could now be seen that stood atop the mighty hill, with a tiny shack erected just beside it.

"There it must lie!" thought The Man with Twenty Fingers, "My answer..."

He continued to heave his weight up the hill, taking large lunges to shorten the time of his journey until at last he stood at its peak. From here, the details of the tree could be witnessed and the clarity of the shack was revealed.

The tree looked like any ordinary tree, with protruding roots at its base, a thick trunk for its center, and webbed branches for its top that sheltered both fruit and shade.

The shack looked even more uneventful, made of wood with no paint, not a single window held within its frame, and a simple door coupled with a rusted pull-handle.

The Man with Twenty Fingers, having seen what awaited ahead of him, turned around to observe what now rested behind...and he felt his breath taken away from the sight.

For, from up so high at the top of this hill, The Man could see everything: the Hospital near the intersection where his mother gave birth to him, the school where he bore his childhood alone and experienced the lashes of his bullies, the apartment he called home where he received the mysterious note, the streets and buildings of the city rising out of the concrete ground in a manmade jigsaw puzzle, where he encountered the Butcher, the Florist, the Innkeeper, the Inn's Resident, the Cat, the Groundskeeper, the little Girl, the Mourning Husband, and the Cryptid.

He saw it all from this height: the path it took to get here, the people he encountered along the way, the sections of weather in the sky and how they changed upon the places which they ruled over— it was all revealed to him from this newfound perspective.

He wondered for a brief instant if any of the others could see him from where he now stood, but the idea fleeted as quick as it arrived, for he knew that along his journey, he never once saw the tall hill standing in the distance. His destination was never visible from afar, but its route was visible from the arrival.

He wondered if everyone down there and everyone he interacted with were aware of just how connected to each other they all were. How they were a mere street away from each other, or a block, or a walk, or a greeting, or a helping hand. And though they were all so clear to him from this perspective, they also now felt the most distant, like one revisiting memories in hindsight.

The Man with Twenty Fingers took a deep breath and let it all go, taking in his last scan of everyone and everything from atop that mighty hill before turning around and approaching the tiny shack to finish this long journey he started.

"Hey there," said a voice from behind the ordinary tree,
"It's nice to meet another so high who's attained this
view to share."

The Man looked over his shoulder and noticed there was an interesting looking figure who sat behind the ordinary tree, obscuring his presence to anyone who climbed the hill head on, but becoming visible once aligned with the shack.

The Man with Twenty Fingers politely smiled and greeted him back.

"Hello there, dear Stranger, it's nice to meet you.
I thought I was alone on this hill, but I guess there are two."

The Stranger then stood up and came out from the shade of the tree and into the sunlight, revealing an ordinary man, with an ordinary face, and an ordinary body, but with one small difference— upon his forehead existed another eye, an extra eye, similar to how The Man had an extra finger.

But something was off about this extra eye — the third one that lay at the center of his forehead — as it looked infected and was closed shut with dried excrement, sealing its lids together.

"So I guess you're here to find your answer, after all,
this is W Hier Yionae Tudare Dr.
Congratulations Reed Doyar Raue, I'm glad you have arrived.
Indeed your hunch has guided you well,
for what you seek is in the shack.
But remember this, and remember it well: once the truth is
revealed, it is futile to look back."

"Thank you, dear Stranger, for the words and the praise.
But might I ask you one question before I go on my way?
That eye of yours, it isn't healthy, why ever is it shut?
And just like my hunch, I know I am right,
for this was told by my gut."

"You're right, Reed Doyar Raue, this eye of
mine should be open wide.
It started out with me rubbing it one day when it felt a little dry.
But after which, it started to hurt, for you see
my fingers are not clean.

Infected it became, encrusted it gained,
glued forever shut it would seem.
Should I ever want to open it, I must scrape off this crap,
But my dirty fingers will only make it worse,
creating an endless trap."

"Well I have an idea, if you'd hear me out,
on how this problem can be solved.
Take this, my finger, and use it instead, and
watch your problems dissolve.
My hands are clean, the cleanest I know,
so trust me if you would,
Use my finger to clean your dirty eye,
and it should solve your problem for good."

The Man with Twenty Fingers then parted with another append-age, and handed it to the Stranger. The Stranger took the finger, ever grateful, ever thankful, ever appreciative, and used it to clear his eye of the infected gunk. To his surprise, more did not regrow as the finger truly was clean, and for the first time in a long time, the stranger was able to open his third eye.

The Man then said his goodbyes to the Stranger and headed into the tiny shack.

The interior of the shack was quite peculiar and caught The Man off guard. It was an empty room of the same old wood exterior, with nothing inside but a door.

However, this door was different from the rest of the shack, as it was pure black with gold decals decorating all around its edges, and tucked in its center right side was a knob made of a pure iridescent material, like that of mother-of-pearl.

"This must be it then, beyond that beautiful door." thought The Man with Twenty Fingers.

And so he reached out to grab and twist the handle, but stopped midway in his tracks.

The Man with Twenty fingers could not believe what he saw, for he noticed that only five fingers existed on each of his hands when he went to grab the knob.

The Man with Twenty Fingers realized he was no longer the man with twenty fingers, but was now only Reed Doyar Raue. He had given away all of them, every single extra finger he ever owned, to the people in need who he encountered along his journey. Gone was the shame, the guilt, the self-hate, the embarrassment, the loathing and spite. Reed Doyar Raue was finally normal. For the first time since his birth, he could confidently call himself that, and to anyone he would ever engage with, they, too, would call him the same.

Confused but happy, ecstatic but hesitant, Reed Doyar Raue had no idea how to react to this discovery.

But, with brand new hands bearing only five fingers, he thought the best thing he could do was *use* them, as a man reborn, a normal person at last, and so he opened the door.

It was a dark room on the other side of that door, but in a carefully considered way. This was no void, but rather a work of art, the magical space within this room.

Black velvet material lined all four of the walls, absorbing most and any light that struck it, while simultaneously reflecting back a sheen of its own — like the moon would the sun's light. The room itself was tiny, no bigger than a closet, with just enough space for Reed Doyar Raue to stand inside of it along with the other two contents that stood there with him.

There was an old antique table, hand carved with care and mysticism, standing at the center, and though it was a beauty, it was not the main attraction. For, upon that table draped a red velvet table cloth, and sat atop that was uniquely shaped box. A long thin candle sat in a silver tray beside the box, its wick producing a gentle glowing flame at its tip, bearing the only source of light in the room. Though the light of this candle struck awe with its mere delicate and perfect existence, it was incomparable to the unequalled box which its rays fell grandiosely on.

Reed Doyar Raue took a step forward, faced the table, and looked down at the box. He then hunched over, picked it up, and began to investigate it.

It was a unique little box, one that unquestionably contained his answer within it. He noticed it required no key to open, but was still controlled by a mysterious mechanic that kept it locked. Twenty holes were drilled into the casing; they had to be pushed down on, then dragged inward to unlock the device in order to open and acquire the treasures within…twenty fingers, that is, acting in unison to open.

Reed Doyar Raue put the box down and stepped back. What is this? Was this a game? What is this "ending" to all that had passed?

How could he arrive at what was supposedly his answer and now not be able to retrieve it?

But, with these questions came specters of deeper thoughts as well, ones that forced Reed Doyar Raue to question himself more than the box. For his whole life, Reed Doyar Raue wished only to be normal. For so long he wished it that he turned it to his dream. That blissful dream to no longer have twenty fingers. That blissful dream to shake hands, hold hands, give a helping hand, and have his hands be noticed with only ten fingers, five on each palm. And now, he finally had that dream, a dream that was once a wish, after all these years, and after all the pain he had to experience that led him to this moment.

Reed Doyar Raue now wondered what his question really was. This whole time, he was journeying to find his answer, but never really gave thought to what question he was finding the answer for.

Did that mean… this was a part of it? This was expected and planned? For, to have his question answered ultimately meant that he would never be able to open this box, as only someone with twenty fingers could unlock this mechanism, and anyone who didn't have such a means was considered normal.

Did this mean what he always, *truly* wanted in life… was to not be able to open this box?

But then, what was the answer within the box? What kind of truth lied hidden within this box's contents? Was his *real* answer within the box, but now he was simply no longer in a capable enough position to open it?

He thought to himself what it would have been like to still have his twenty fingers and be able to open this box.

Would such a thing even be able to satisfy him anymore? Because, to be in such a position to open it would mean he would have knowingly abandoned all of the people in need who he came across during his journey, people he only came across *because* of this journey.

Reed Doyar Raue had gotten his wish, acquired his dream, but were those the same as his answer? Were they two separate things, or were they always one in the same?

A single sentence pervaded his frenzied mind through this internal conflict, lingering in the back of his consciousness like the bitterness of a lime makes refuge on the back of the tongue. In constant repeat, during this ever growing enigmatic epiphany which Reed Doyar Raue was currently experiencing, those words from the Stranger back at the tree kept entering his head, the one with three eyes, stationed outside the shack "…Once the truth is revealed, it is futile to look back."

A MASK MADE OF GOLD, SILVER AND PLATINUM

Annabelle the Petite. The whispered name and accompanied title now echoed faintly like a light draft in the endless void, almost forgotten if not for the shred of its utterance that still continued to ripple out, seething into the endless abyss where it was once spoken but now faded.

None of the runts or scavengers that roamed this plane of existence knew of its origin, nor what dimension it stemmed from when it fell into the Oblivion Mother, who adopts all that has been abandoned or forgotten with time. To them, it was just another passing of a life, another fable dismissed, another history left untouched like the rest of the matter, life, and essence that has become lost within this realm.

But what a tale those runts and scavengers would find if they chose to follow its thread, a tale that most beings across most dimensions could benefit from and perhaps even find a power in. A power that could have prevented them from ever winding up in such a land of dismay.

For the story of Annabelle the Petite is just that; rooted in one who was once crushed by the soles of a false prophet, an appointed force, but discovered the truth of power only visible from under the oppressive feet of a liar.

Her name may occupy the Oblivion Mother's domain, but *she* does not, and to bear ears to her story means we must start at a time before she acquired the accompanied title.

A time before Annabelle had any power... in fact, when she had none.

Her story takes place in a barren land where the sky was laced with a hue of scarlet, and the ground was embedded with a shade of rust. The air itself was thick and heavy— weighing down the lungs of its inhaler with a painful expansion, followed by a tardy expelling of its overt density, leaking out of their mouths like rich molasses and abandoning them with a gasping desperation for their next breath, maintaining this sadistic cycle.

Storms were harsh but few, making water just as rare as food. This in turn, made any habitable champaign that was free from the harsh lashes of nature or the perverse hunger of animals, almost always bearing a fruitless livelihood.

This constant dearth was the way of life in this twisted reality, and the worst part of it all was that despite the struggle one would have to endure to survive, and the lack resources that existed at almost all points of location, life never ceased to constantly sprout into this accursed world.

Desolate was not the word to describe this tormented plane in space, but rather, *agony.*

And like an old tune of madness that always slithers out of the fool's pipe; the cruel found a way to rule, the vile found a way to thrive, the evil found a means to be fat, and the despicable possessed a mercy which they never handed out.

Annabelle had lived in these lands for twenty three years. Although her village contained occupants who were far older or far younger, it was still an impressive feat that she had survived long enough to reach such an age, for the susceptibility to death had plateaued at its peak for everyone at the moment of their conception.

Within her village, life was quite different from how we, *the observers* from outside her realm, are accustomed to viewing a community working and living together.

This world was scarce in all its necessitates for sustaining and nurturing life, remember? So of course, the lifestyles and duties of their shared existence in their small village held no real sense of community.

Because water almost never made its dampening mark from the skies to the earth, and since the soil was burdened with the same cruelty and dry existence as the animate life on it, no one was the appointed farmer for the village and its people.

Instead, they all had fenced segments of land outside of their homes, littered with seeds from wherever they could be found, waiting dormant for the miracle of a single passing of rain to raise them from their beds.

Because resources were scarce, no one was the assigned tailor or weaver of wools, linen, and cotton for the village. Instead, they all made their own clothes within their own families and households, using old scraps of cloth from the garments now outgrown or from looting apparel off of the unfortunate, but all too common, deceased neighbor lying cold in the road or in their home.

As you can see by now, this community was almost anything but a community, with each resident and household forced into an independent existence by this frugal dimension.

So why did these people form together? Why did they build their houses one by one next to each other, their empty gardens shoulder-to-shoulder in front of their homes? What was the reason for their creation of roads, their attempts at wells, and their construction of the tall stone border that surrounded their little village— all of this being done under the unusual proposition of pooling their resources and working together?

Well, to put it simply, because they are human. And humans, those strange and fickle creatures, do love company. They prefer it in times of joy, in times of sorrow, in times of fear, in times of suffering, and even in their single moments near death.

Humans just happen to like to share, not so much the material and physical, but the abstract things that encompass the *experience* of life.

However, that company they crave is by no means limited to other humans, and some brave souls have even dared to reach out to a higher power in those lonely moments, calling down the deities we revere as gods for consolation.

Within Annabelle's local lands, only one man was known for having done such a thing, and soon she found herself on a pilgrimage to meet with that very man turned ruler, embarking with a handful of others from her village to the King of the Red Castle, where they planned to beg for food on behalf of their starving families.

She, like the others in her company, had never left the territory that bound their homes together, since only death awaited outside their community. But a Black horse had trotted through their village in recent times, bringing a famine into their lives that eradicated the sustenance that even the will-to-survive was once able to fill. What was once the *pains* of hunger was now the *consequences*.

As Annabelle and the others walked on the long road in a tight herd-like grouping, venturing beyond the protection of their village's stone border and towards the center of these vast lands, they gossiped and exchanged all manners of rumors they had acquired over the years about the Red Castle and its King.

They spoke of how he was chosen by the gods to be their single voice to man in this world riddled with anguish. How he was so beautiful, the gods gave him a mask decorated with precious metals to wear, so that other humans wouldn't compare his beauty to theirs. How he had grown into a giant of a human over time from the power of the gods' voices constantly being casted through him. How his castle was once the home of the gods, made by their very hands from a time when they once roamed this earth, but left it to him once they too saw the decaying order of this world.

Giddy with the thoughts of silencing the aching gnaws of hunger they hosted in their bellies, they passed these stories on through smiling faces as they traveled to what they destined was their new salvation.

It took many suns and even more moons, but eventually, Annabelle and the others in her pilgrimage finally reached the estate that housed the grand palace, who's structure had only occupied the fantasies of their minds and the offsprings of their imaginations until now— the Red Castle.

But with a shuffle of discomfort and a shared timid hesitance, the Red Castle disturbed them as it was nothing like they had expected it to be.

It was the single most prodigious construction they had ever seen in their life, with nothing capable of even coming close to its grandeur. Large slabs of crimson stones were bonded and stacked on top of each other, some pieces the size of monoliths, shaping the majestic architecture of the Red Castle; displaying six visible towers from the front and all of them bearing flags, two drum towers visible from the front as well that jutted from its outer wall, the gatehouse of the inner wall erecting from higher behind the front wall, and the colossal, fortified keep — protruding higher and more regal than any other feature of the castle.

However, the awe evoked by the imposing presence of the Red Castle was undoubtedly corrupted by a malevolent essence that seeped subtly through the tiny details riddled amongst its structure.

Thick, iron bands wrapped around any circular architecture, including the towers and the pillars on top of the keep, with large round bolts hammered in, holding the metallic rings in place.

Countless spikes were tapered at the end of a majority of the castle's tall features, shaping into long sharp points, uncannily thin, as if it were not created for the purpose of a powerful, royal aesthetic, but rather to impale an unknown force that could strike down from the sky.

The flags boasted on their wooden poles were battered and torn, having not held up well nor been replaced over generations, losing in a long and slow battle against the wind.

The large gate that posed as the entrance to the Red Castle filled up half of the outer wall in height, bearing welded spikes on its caged metal, facing outwards to keep the unwanted away... but also inward to keep some inside.

Nonetheless, with loved ones back home at their village either dying or on the brink of death, along with the extreme hunger they had worked up for themselves from the travel just endured, such a minor inconvenience like a nefarious note of suspicion was nowhere near enough to deter them from continuing onwards.

As Annabelle and the others approached the great gate, they were intervened by several guards who stood watch at its entrance.

They too carried an intimidating aspect in their visual representation, as they were cladded in uniforms made of a rough, red-tanned leather. The leather was discomfortingly thick, bringing into question what manner of beast bore this flesh at a time before it was ripped, clipped, skinned and fashioned as a suit of protection for these servants. It was covered with iron studs and had large creases in the areas that were exposed to the most movement, along with shallow splits from the failed slashes of perpetrators and the violent clashes from invasions.

The guards also carried an array of weapons, making it known that their uniforms may have been restricted by a code, but not their preference of killing.

One had a jagged sword at his waist, serrated not by the hands of a blacksmith, but of a natural chipping from its barbaric use.

Another held onto a spear, holding it up-right at attention, pointing towards the sky. It looked as though it had never once been cleaned, with what must have been dozens of victims' blood bleached into the upper shaft near the spear's head. This gave it the illusion of an encrusting rust, while scraps and strings of various colored fabrics dangled from the splinters of its wooden shaft.

And the third and last one clung onto a battle-ax, its head being double-ended for easier slaughter, and its decapitating weight made apparent by the mere stance the guard had to brace just to hold it.

"Halt no further, scattered souls" said the guard bearing the serrated sword, making his lead amongst the other soldiers apparent. His voice sounded nothing like Annabelle expected, as it was greatly aged in comparison to his facial features, and carried a drowned crackle at the end of each breath. "Before you stands the Red Castle, home to our King, Borris the Great Voice, ruler of all land within sight of this forte. If you've come seeking aid, shelter, food, or communion with the gods, then you may enter now and find council with the King. If your matter is another, speak it now to our company— Borris the Great Voice will not reckon any other affairs unless debriefed of it through us."

Annabelle and the others stated their desires for food and were promptly escorted into the Red Castle with no more issues or added interruptions.

It seemed strange to her though that finding entrance proved relatively easy, especially with how many hungry mouths were in her party. How the designated ones immediately let in were those who sought some form of a giving hand, and the rejected ones blocked of entry were those who sought anything else. She struggled to think of exactly what else one could possibly come here for if not for a handout, and why everything but charity was restricted from passage by an intervention of the guards first.

But perhaps... it wasn't all as odd as it seemed. Annabelle may have been poor, but she was very self-aware. She knew the customs of her village may not define the same customs of those elsewhere. She too had felt the slight cold nature from the separation of each family's home life in her village, despite their close proximity as neighbors. She had already figured that some lands might have received more rain, grown better crops, or produced better clothes, and the Red Castle had done nothing to her in the moment but prove that.

With a palace like this, leathered clothes as the common uniform, and a conjunction with the gods, perhaps generosity was an ordinary disposition here. She had already taken into account that her own life experience may have placed her into a position of misjudgment here.

And so, she held onto this optimistic ideology as the guards led them inside the keep, eventually reaching two tall doors manned by even more armed men, who pushed them open where a booming voiced ushered their entry before they could even bear witness to what lied on the other side.

"Ah! More, more, more! Come in, come in. Approach thee, I, King Borris the Great Voice, the Ambassador of the Gods' Will, the Plentiful and the Generous, Owner of all Lands under the Red

Castle's Shadow! Beseech my help and lay forward your gratitude, your offerings, your worship, and yourselves. Come now, line up in front of my table, let me see your faces and hear your prayers."

In a large room where the ceiling couldn't be seen for how endlessly high up it went, lied a large table that stretched almost from wall to wall with a feast of innumerous fruits, vegetables, cooked beasts, baked breads, and crafted pastries resting atop its surface. The room was filled with an intimidating number of men who wore the same hide-armor and carried similar cruel weapons to the previous guards at the gate's entrance. And at the very back of the room protruded a large throne from the floor directly opposite to the doors entrance, where an even larger man sat upon its seat.

The sight of this gargantuan individual took away all of Annabelle's attention from the food. This man was a giant, scaling twenty feet in height and accompanied by the same width in fat. He was an elephantine birthed of pure gluttony, a size only achieved by a never-ending consumption of food and drink.

It was terrifying to behold this man, his proportions not nearing anything that is human. If she had to compare, his size was relative to that of the front gates of the Red Castle where the guards first stopped them, only the King was more round and bulbous in his shape.

The power and threatening presence that reeked off this colossal of a man was no different than the unnerving impression one gets when standing before a great boulder carved out of the mountains— an imposing pressure by just the sheer overwhelmingness of its stationary existence.

This King, Borris the Great Voice, was not dressed in leather like the rest of his men however, but instead wore a majestic robe made of what must have been a felt material, shimmering with a midnight blue color as white rippling ruffles lined all throughout its edges.

He did not carry any kind of weapon like his men, but instead, wore a mask on his face, one made of gold, silver, and platinum. It interchanged between the precious metals with its gilded designs and magnificent decals, patterned gracefully in unison upon the natural flow and angles of the mask's face shape.

The mask bore only three holes: two for the eyes and a slight crevice for the mouth.

Annabelle could faintly see the King's eyes peering from behind the mask. They looked bloodshot and strained, making their gentle blue iris' not a foundation of beauty, but rather of a revolting yearn in pig like hunger.

"From where do you creatures come?" asked the King, an air of condescendence woven intricately into his words.

"We come from a small village about fi—" one within Annabelle's party began to speak but was swiftly interrupted by King Borris the Great Voice, who now seemed impatient and on the verge of rage.

"From where do you come?" he asked once more, a tension setting into the occupied room, creating a difference in the aura of the guards as if they had experienced this often and knew of their next actions to take should the presented party not satisfy their King.

"From East, King Borris the Great Voice" answered Annabelle before anyone else could speak out, knowing exactly what the King meant by his question.

And this proved to be true, as the King then settled back into his throne while the atmosphere dissipated its previous tension.

"Ah, the East!" the King's voice sounded lighter and almost intrigued by Annabelle's response, continuing on the topic nonchalantly as if their homeland was a mere playing piece in a game to him, "Let's see, last I checked, the North had a White horse trot through their lands.

They came to me for aid like you all do now. And with this mask I wear, gifted to me by the gods on behalf of their divinity, I spoke with them and beckoned their will, to which they granted my interference!

I spared as much as I could to help the North defeat their invaders, giving food, wealth, weapons and soldiers to their cause. They won of course, with my help, for it was the will of the gods! And now they send me great gifts of thanks— take a look at my table before you, notice the animals not of this region? They are Northern! Exotic and exquisite.

Hmm, and then a Red horse trotted its hooves through the South, happening to make its way up here, to me. The South followed it, angry at my obstructing hand in their Northern conquest.

They brought war to my door, perverting my lands with their men and their havoc.

Of course, with the gods on my side, their little fit of a war ended as fast as it began. Depleted of soldiers, depleted of food, depleted of resources, they had almost nothing left after our little war, besides of course, that vast amount of land they called the South.

They too, after having pointed their blades at me, knelt their bodies at my feet and begged for my aid. It was a scary thought indeed, what the North might do to those who once tried to conquer their lands but were now too weak to protect their own.

And after calling out to my glorious gods and crying for their answer, I received their instructions and took in the poor South as though it were my own land. Their people became under my protection and belonged to me now, so no scary Northerners could dare harm them or retaliate against them for their past crimes."

Borris the Great Voice took a pause and let out a deep sigh from his belly, "Of course, there *was* the West. Oh how sad, it pains my heart, but a Pale horse crossed through their lands. I had only interacted with them once before such a tragedy struck their lives.

They came to me different from all of the others… different from yourselves.

They didn't seek my aid.

They weren't at war or being conquered, nor were they starving or experiencing any form of danger. It puzzled me at first, but then they informed me of their lives.

They were happy. They were safe. They had plenty of rain and crops and materials for shelter and clothes. They had no enemies nor did they make any. They prospered in their Western lands.

And so, they had no interest in me… nor the gods. They rejected any contact or conversation I offered them with the mighty beings, the old rulers of this world, the divine souls of everlasting mercy and raw power."

The King lowered his head and spoke softly after, "And yet, with all that life, a Pale horse managed to cross through their lands.

No doubt, they offended the gods by not seeking their council, by believing themselves to be better than the divine beings, for thinking they were exempt from their wishes and guidance just because their existence was fruitful."

Borris the Great Voice raised his head and scanned the party now before him, and though Annabelle could not see his mouth, his eyes told her of his smile behind the mask, "Death scoured their lands from no source that I can tell of. And so… naturally, I sent my new brethren of the South across our vast plains to acquire those plentiful resources the Westerners spoke of, bringing the riches from there to here. Everything that was good of the West is now everything that is good of here, through my lap they land on the laps of the gods!"

He began to shuffle around, propping himself up against the arms of the throne-chair into a better posture, sitting more upright in his throne while causing a great rustle in the process. Like a tempest in the woods, the noise of his movements echoed off the walls from his immense size.

"So, what horse hath trotted through the East? Hmm?" he asked.

"Black" answered Annabelle, already feeling responsible for ensuring her party's success in their quest for the King's salvation, especially after the last near-fatal interaction incited by one in her company.

"Black… I see" he said beginning to laugh, entertained by the idea, "How cruel of me to have such a feast set in front of all you people, on my table. You must be famished, I imagine. My previous speech and introduction must have not even reached your ears over the rumble in your stomachs and the instinct of your lurking eyes."

Some people within the party began to nod honestly, while others remained still, having not taken their gaze off the food since they entered the room.

"Well then! Come! Come! Approach me one by one, please. I shall hear your prayers and deliver them on to the gods, and once they receive those nurturing tears of yours, they shall relay their answer through me. Come! Come!"

From the line they had formed horizontally, shoulder-to-shoulder upon their initial entry, they now maintained as they walked around the table of feasts and lined up in a vertical order to present themselves to the King.

Upon their turn, each person would kneel before Borris the Great Voice, looking down at the ground while they made their request as to look up at him from such a position was impossible for the anatomy of the human neck.

Some would ask for food. Some would ask for food for their family. Some asked for food immediately, and some asked for food to last them an entire year or a lifetime.

The King's process went like so; he would listen to their request and then close his eyes, gradually emitting strange noises. Whispers, grunts, moans and sometimes even speaking in tongues, he tossed his head side to side as the mask which linked him across different dimensions to the where the gods resided took full affect. He'd heed their words, something no one else within the magnificent throne room could hear besides him, before ceasing all his movements and noise, then, looking down upon the poor soul begging for his aid, he'd convey the decision of the gods.

For each person that went, two things always happened no matter what they asked; King Borris the Great Voice would refer to them in a demeaning fashion having no name to address them by, such as hag, pest, dog, mongrel, beggar, scum, dirt, ect.— and he would always give them what they wanted, exactly what they wanted, to the fullest degree since the gods had told him to do so.

When it was finally Annabelle's turn, she approached the King in the same manner which everyone else had done, kneeling before him, head to the ground, and spoke aloud what she sought.

"King Borris the Great Voice, I wish food for me and my family back home. I have a mother, a father, and a younger brother. My request is enough food necessary for my brother to holdfast to life and never fall to death by any means of starvation."

Annabelle was then caught off-guard when the King asked her something that he had not asked of the others.

"What is your name?"

"Annabelle, King Borris the Great Voice."

"Annabelle… *Annabelle the Petite.* You remind me of myself, did you know that? The way you speak for these people in your party, the people from your village. They are like a lost herd of sheep, brainless and clueless, likely to have perished had you not spoken up.

But you know that, don't you? 'Tis the very reason why you did.

I too, act as a voice for the weak. I speak to the gods—" he pointed up into the air, "On behalf of man.

Man is too weak, too naive to have contact with the gods. They may say the wrong things, ask the wrong questions, give the wrong answers, and anger the gods. That is why I speak on their behalf, *your* behalf.

We are shepherds to these pitiful souls, are we not?"

Annabelle said nothing.

"Hmm, nevertheless, I have another question for you, Annabelle the Petite. This village you come from, and the lands of the East which it's cradled in— what does it offer?"

"...I'm sorry... I— I don't understand?"

"The East! Your village! What luxuries are produced from its soil? Or what crafts are created by its people? What does the East have to offer me?"

"Nothing, your King. The East's soil has no yield. We people have nothing. We don't even have each other.

Death and hunger are all that roam the terrain of the East.

Light hast cast a sheen over the Black horse's coat, reflecting a white glare back, turning the once Black horse, Pale. We come here to you now for your grace and the blessings of the gods... to save us from it all."

Though Annabelle could not see it for her eyes were fixed on the ground, the King's eyes behind his mask slouched heavy behind their lids to this news.

"Nothing. The East has nothing to offer? You... have nothing to offer? Is that why you all appear before me with dark sunken eyes? Is that why not a single bone within any of you lies hidden with some courtesy behind fat? Is that why you all wear tattered rags, displeasingly sewn together, and reek of sweat, decay, and a revolting odor? Is that why you wear no shoes, but only socks, blooded and dirtied and torn from you travel here? Is that why none of you have been blessed with rain for a proper bathing, and your hair is matted to your heads from years of oil and debris?

You bring your filth, along with your pitiful existences, into my kingdom, my domain, my lands, my castle, my presence, with nothing to offer, yet expect me to find mercy from the gods on your behalf!?"

Again, Annabelle said nothing.

"...The gods will not like what I have to tell them now. Pray while I commune with them on your request, for they shall not be happy with this new information."

Annabelle's body began to shake like a stray dog's, but she did everything within her power to control the fear that now rattled and compromised her composure.

King Borris the Great Voice began his convulsions and whispers, however, they lasted far shorter than they had with any other person that went before her. And when he spoke to her after, he had the same monotone voice he had when telling her to pray just moments before, empty of any divinity or exalting energy.

"No. You may have nothing.

They said 'one like you, who has a voice and a power to speak up for others, should be more than fine in acquiring food for themselves, or for your family if you so dire'.

If you are not too weak enough to be your party's voice, then you should easily be able to find yourself a solution for your hunger as well. Perhaps during such a trial of exercising capability, you may also find something along the way that the East has to offer the gods. Now go."

The trembling flow in Annabelle's body intensified, and her heart beat so hard she could feel it in her throat.

She was caught off-guard by the sudden realization that she was in fact, talking back to the King in that moment. She could faintly hear what she was saying as her pounding heart reached even her eardrums, and the whole moment felt like it was happening outside of her body. To her, it felt like she was just being carried along through it all, like an infant suckling its mother's tit during her daily chores, having no control in the motion of things that was occurring around it.

"No!" she begged, "Please! My brother, he can't— he *won't* be able to go any longer without food! He will die soon. He'll starve! Please, I beg you, ask the gods again! Beg them! I beg you! They must be wrong, there's no way—"

"Quiet!" boomed the order from the King. His shout erupted from his belly and bounced off the walls in a fury.

His anger, his *power*, frightened Annabelle so much, that a warm leaking sensation spread down from her inner thighs and dampened the tops of her red and brown stained socks.

"How dare you! You whore! You filthy peasant! Mongrel!

How dare you question the gods and their decision!? Who are you, you tiny human, with the value of a flea, to question my voice? My holy conversation with the almighty beings who know all and everything?

Seize her! Take this dirty whore and throw her in prison! I want her to feel the disgrace and disgust of darkness— an utter abandonment from the very gods which she so unruly questioned and doubted so!

Abandon all hope, Annabelle the Petite, for this is the will of the gods!"

Annabelle struggled to plea her case, to ask for mercy, to right her wrong… but it mattered not. The loyal, yet despicable guards of the King, jumped on her like dogs and dragged her out of the throne room.

She kicked and screamed and scratched and fought, but none seemed to loosen the grips of the guards on her, nor slow their descent down into the deep, sunken dungeons in the bowel of the Red Castle.

She was tossed discriminately into a tiny, cobbled-wall cell, and scraped open her flesh upon impact with the floor. The ground was moist, the air was infected with mold and suffering, and there were no window nor any bars to let in even the smallest amount of light.

All that existed inside this tiny chamber besides Annabelle, was a single bucket in the corner of its space for all of her private necessities.

The truth was, Annabelle knew her fate had been decided the moment that iron door was shut behind her, encasing her in darkness. She did not scream nor fight any longer. Instead, she just curled up into a ball on the ground, attempting to achieve any means of comfort or warmth that she could find in that fetal position, and awaited the death that couldn't be too far away.

But how wrong she was, for King Borris the Great Voice had no intention of letting her slowly rot dead in that dark and silence, no. He had other plans for her, bigger plans, plans of horrors which she was soon to discover only mere hours into her entrapment.

No different than the soldiers he had at the sides of his throne, or the guards he had at his castle's gate, or the people of the South who he had at his disposal, King Borris the Great Voice had many torturers in his dungeon as well, and poor Annabelle was destined to meet them all.

Her first encounter came from the buckets of freezing ice. They disturbed her moments of coping with the situation, as the guards would swiftly open the door to her cell and splash the frigid waters against her body.

Thin layers of ice that had formed at the top of the bucket's contents would break upon hitting her skin, causing tiny cuts to open on her flesh and allow the water to reach even deeper inside her.

Then came the man who ripped and tore her nails. It felt as though the torturer had a fixation with the hands and feet, as he would always caress her appendages in a caring manner, handling them gently and delicately before clamping down on the nails and pulling, wiggling, twisting, then tugging them out from their bed of attachment.

Once all of her fingers and toes only produced their fleshly, soft pulps, she was then handled by a different torturer who would shove her head into a troff of water.

She would struggle and fight her way to bring her head back up, ignoring the pain or blood this caused her nail-less hands to endure.

Her head would remain under the water until she eventually lost consciousness. She never remembered being pulled out— but only being shoved back in the moment she regained her bearings and could finally breathe once again.

Whether this next one was the cook or an actual torturer, Annabelle could not tell, for he would force her into a tiny cage which he would then lower into a pot of boiling oil.

Annabelle lost her voice to scream during this method, letting out only pitiful chirp-like sounds similar to a bird, while her throat experienced an agonizing pain in itself, on the verge of prolapsing.

And so this went on and on with every torturer she was introduced to. One laid her on a wooden table and stretched her limbs from their joints. Another tied her to a chair and prodded her with a glowing hot poker. While one torturer would hammer her hands, another one would pull out her teeth.

Though Annabelle could not ascertain the amount time which had passed from within her dark prison, nor while basking in the endless currents of pain from the dungeon's systematic torment, it had actually been a full three months since she had last seen the light of day, or experienced an existence without this needless suffering.

Once again, Annabelle lie cradled in her own arms on the wet ground of her tiny cell, disassociated with the world and the space around her, death no further away than the throne room atop all those spiraling stair steps above her.

This torture, this darkness, this hopelessness and this unending agony… surely the gods would understand and have mercy on Annabelle if she could speak to them herself. Surely they would listen and gain a knew perspective on the matter if *she* held the communion with them. But alas, she did not have the mask to do so. Only the King on his throne carried the means to initiate contact with the gods, and having been the very one to put her down here, he was not going to hand it over to allow Annabelle a chance to plead on her own behalf.

She knew she couldn't steal it, for there was no way she could escape. Not with the arrangement of this tiny prison's security, and certainly not with her beaten and broken body.

So, if Annabelle was to have any chance of communicating with the gods, then she would need to make a mask of her own.

However, she possessed neither precious metals to fashion the mask from, nor any valuable gems to decorate its face with. There was nothing she could use that would glorify and honor such mighty and powerful beings.

All Annabelle had… was a bucket. A bucket filled with feces, bile, and menstrual blood.

The contents within that bucket were an account of all her time spent there in that wretched cell, represented in a physical form of matter— all the shit from the maggots and insect eggs they fed her, which barely kept her alive. All the bile from her body's regurgitation, a response brought on by the rupturing of her organs during torture. And lastly, all the blood from the many cycles she was forced to endure while in these unfavorable conditions, some even brought on early from the sadistic methods that the torturers used.

Annabelle couldn't recall when she had the actual thought, nor what made her think of it in the first place. There was no guarantee of its success in working, nor anything prompting her attempt, but she tried it nonetheless.

Annabelle dipped her hands into the putrid slush contained within the bucket and smeared it onto her face.

She continued this process of scooping out the contents and wiping them all over her face for hours, whispering and crying and begging and praying, either aloud or in her head… until at last… something spoke out to her.

"I hear you, my child" came a voice from all around her yet nowhere at all.

There was no true way to describe the sound of the voice, for it was not a voice at all, really. Like when one has thoughts in their own head, or sounds out a word in the silent privacy of their mind, it had a clear voice just as much as it didn't.

Annabelle ceased her ritual, freezing in place from the surprise of the sudden voice that answered her prayers.

"Abandon all fear, dear child" said the voice as if it were aware of her emotion and shock, "For your tiny soul can not comprehend my true essence. You'll never arrive at the fullest understanding to respectfully show fear for my being. And should your awareness ever grow to be capable of such a thing, your soul will have still not achieved an evolution to attain the full capacity to fill that order. 'Tis a needless effort, so abandon all fear."

Strangely, Annabelle understood the message that this… being… was trying to convey, and felt an instant flush of relief fall over her.

"Who—who are you?" she asked, "Are you one of the gods I seek to speak with."

"No, child. I am not one of them, for they do not exist."

"Do not exist?"

"I have now seen the entirety of your world, this realm which you have beckoned me to, in the moment I heard and answered your call. This domain is a plague, and I am sorry your soul was caught by its net in the sea of the universe when your essence found conception. But no god nor any gods have ever touched this land. 'Tis why only suffering exists within its life."

"But, who does the King commune with then? Who are the gods that deemed this torment upon me?"

"The King who calls himself Borris the Great Voice, only communes with himself.

He is just another man, dear child. A cruel but clever one at that. Through wicked actions and heartless toil, that man has managed to make even a demented reality like this one, bend to his feet. And now, he has made its people do just the same."

"...So he lied?"

"Oh, he's lied about much more, my child. You are not the first one to have tasted the sharp end of his atrocities. Countless others have, in fact.

However, you are the first one to have called out to me and gained my attention."

"How so? What is so different from my prayers than the countless others who must have whispered in their hearts while their stomachs devoured themselves? Or those who preached to the skies with all their voice when their families or children all collapsed in demise around them?"

"Well, by that beautiful mask of yours, of course."

"The mask? *My* mask? But, its no cause for glory. It has nothing of high honoring or of value to be worthy of any being beyond this world to answer it."

"Oh child, how you are wrong.

Why would I ever turn my attention to a mask made of Gold, Silver, and Platinum? Why would I cast my gaze which sees and overlooks a countless loop of folded infinities and endless spaces of existence, to a prayer casted under a jeweled mask?

What could any small being, who found a means to create and acquire a mask of such value, ever need my aid for? With such a possession, surely they can find a means to attain whatever else they seek in the world they come from.

But a mask like *yours* — so vile and repugnant, distasteful and repulsive — to bear such a crude mask while begging for deliverance… that makes you my child. For only a child can twist the heart of the parent when bearing witness to the pain of that young soul."

"So, does that mean… you are god?"

"I am. But I am not one, for there are many. Some good, some bad, some careless and some careful. Some born, some made, some lost and some forgotten.

And there are many more beings besides gods that roam these spiraling planes, with just as much immense power as well.

The universe is ever and eternal, and so are some of the beings that exist in its never-ending expansion of existence."

Annabelle was able to make sense of everything this god told her. It felt not like new knowledge to her, but of an old one being retold, as if she once knew all this to be true from a time before she came to be… *her now*, so to say.

"Mighty god" she said in a strong voice, confident and aware of the situation and her position within it, "I, your child, seek your helping hand and aid."

"What is it that you seek?"

"I seek strength, mighty god. My broken body repaired. My infected wounds healed. My incapable body made capable."

"What else, my child?" replied the god, as if knowing she had a bigger request, as if *hopping* she had a bigger request.

"I seek power. I wish to break free from this prison I've been shackled in. I wish to kill all who put me in here. I want retribution against all who have tortured me, and against the King of the Red Castle, Borris the Great Voice, who has bestowed a great many barbarities against me and the countless other before me."

"I see" said the god, sounding more pleased.

"And lastly" continued Annabelle, "I seek attunement with you, my god and my parent, so I may leave this accursed dimension. I want to escape this damned reality, and all the worlds and lands that occupy it, never setting foot in realm like it again."

Though the god's presence was known to her only by its voice and nothing visual, she knew it was smiling right now in this moment. She could just *feel* it.

"What is your name, child?" asked the god.

"Annabelle, mighty god. But here, in this place, they call me Annabelle the Petite."

"Annabelle the Petite… Annabelle… I have the means to grant you what you seek.

A matrimony, to bestow a small fragment of my soul unto yours in a rebirth. You will be more, you will be greater, you will be you, and from such— be able to find your true name within your soul that you have long since forgotten… or perhaps, wish to forge anew.

Are you certain this is what you seek. With what I am about to give you, no wall made from that earth can contain you, no man will have the power to subdue you, and no dimension will have the ability to bound you.

You will start anew, not of consciousness, but one of learning, for even demigods are burdened with the deep truths of the universe which simple souls can escape from having to endure.

With that known, do you still want to accept what I have to offer?"

"I do." said Annabelle, without a single trace of hesitance or reluctance in her resolve.

"Well then blink, my child, for it is done."

Annabelle closed her eyes, bidding farewell to that which once made her human, that which once was her humanity, her old soul, un-evolved, a cage in itself, and reopened her eyes anew.

Her bones were mended, wounds were closed, scars gone, blood faded, and her body was strengthened and enforced by a new power.

It was more than healed, it was now more than what she had crawled out from birth with. Though she may have looked the same on the outside, anyone within her presence would say she was anything but.

Annabelle rose to her two feet effortlessly, and put her hand on the prison door.

It burst instantaneously into thousands of splinters that blew out into the opposing wall in a loud eruption.

Immediately, guards and her torturers alike poured out from their rooms and rushed her direction as she slowly strode down the hallways.

All it took was a wave of the hand, a nod of the head, or an expanding stretch of the shoulders for those perpetrators to encounter their demise at Annabelle's will.

They too exploded like the door, or met a unique fate if they had been one the unfortunate souls to have inflicted a special suffering upon her during her time in the prison.

The ones who threw the glacial water on her became paralyzed in space, while countless cuts opened across their bodies and their blood was pulled out of them and into the air, floating weightlessly as though void of all gravity from those cherried slits.

The man who tore her nails out found himself levitating off the ground as his whole body was skinned, layer by layer, down to the core of his bones.

She blew a wisp of air at the man who drowned her over and over again, which entered into his lungs and then burst them in sudden expansion.

The man who boiled her in hot oil found his flesh bubbling and melting from the heat of an invisible flame that caressed his entire body, until all that remained of him was a pile of reduced human liquids.

The one who pulled her limps had all of his appendages, from leg, to arm, to phallus and head, ripped from his torso piece by piece.

He who had poked her with the hot iron was burned through and through by multiple, tiny glowing hot-holes blazing in his flesh.

The one that hammered her hands collapsed inside of himself, twisted and mangled like a rag-doll, as though a blackhole blossomed in his center.

And the one who ripped her teeth out found his mouth inverting on itself, ripping open and folding in like a pillowcase turned inside-out.

Slowly and patiently, like a being beyond the rush of time or the existence of matter itself, Annabelle walked up those spiraling stairs and out of the dungeon. She reached the main housing of the Red Castle's keep, and entered the throne room once again.

It had been three months since she last set foot in this room, back when she was a different being altogether. And once more, she stood across the room from Borris the Great Voice, the circumstances this time catastrophically dissimilar, while his guards flooded in from everywhere to charge at her.

They were all met with the same instant demise as the pitiful minions down below — who's corpses now filled the dungeons — in the exact same fashion of Annabelle barely lifting a finger for their slaughter, not needing to touch them at all.

Soon, the throne room was painted red like the castle's exterior walls, and all that remained in the throne room was Annabelle and the King.

She observed him from where she stood, now able to see him for what he truly was for the first time.

It was as the god had told her, he was nothing more than a human. His size was only from how much he ate, and his power only from the illusion of this great size.

She saw no god or gods encompassing the aura of his being, nor did she sense or feel them with her newfound sight.

Borris the Great Voice was Borris the Great Lie. He had no beings watching over him, contacting him, acting through him, and especially in this case— protecting him.

Annabelle began to approach him, noting how the eyes that once looked down at her with that loathsome, pig-like hunger, were now filled only with terror.

He could not move from his throne, and he could not run nor fight back even if he wanted to. His enormous size now betrayed, a hidden aspect to the false truth which he used as his intimidating power.

This was Borris the Great Lie, and Annabelle needn't use her power to keep him still for her as she approached.

"Now" she said, reaching the foot of his throne, "You kneel."

Borris' body began to make loud crackles and pop sounds, while his eyes morphed into a look of indescribable pain, flooding pink with blood.

These snaps and breaking noises continued to grow louder as his body began to display a physical difference as to what was going on.

The enormous body that was not capable of movement was now beginning to take on a new form. His femurs burst through the caps of his knees, while his spine bent forward causing his entire belly to rupture open and spill all of his innards out onto the floor.

His rib caged folded completely downward, touching his pelvic bone now that none of his organs nor any of his flesh obstructed their contact from each other.

Broken, twisted, and already dead by the end of it all, Borris' head was now touching the ground in front of Annabelle's feet, his monstrous body eternally humbled in the kneeling position before her.

Taking notice of the sparkling glamour that twinkled amongst the gore, Annabelle stooped over his corpse and picked up the mask of lies, once belonging to the now dead king.

"Now I am, and now I see" she said, "Truly, what manner of gods would ever answer a calling to such a mask?" wondered Annabelle.

"Indeed" responded the mighty god, "And in the glorious yet frightful way of the universe, you are now such a being that the wearer of such a mask would hope to beckon."

Annabelle studied the mask's details, "Should I cast this out of this realm? So no other human may make the same arrangement of lies as this one did. Though I know now the truth, any lesser being can still fall fool for its symbolism under a false prophet."

"You could" answered the mighty god, "And I suggest you do whatever you like.

However... I say *you* wear it.

For of all things it suits now, I say it suits you best. Whatever else could be great enough to adorn such a mask, if not you?"

Annabelle remained staring at it for a couple moments longer, before proceeding to slip its casting upon her face.

"And remember" continued the mighty god, "the house is just as much a symbol as the mask which it beholds at its alter.

Finish up there and then come to me. There is much beauty to be seen outside of that maledict dimension you're in."

Annabelle turned towards the entrance and proceeded to gracefully walk out of the throne room, and then the keep, and then the Red Castle all together.

As she stepped out onto its gate's edge and the land which bordered it, the Red Castle collapsed and crumbled, leaving nothing of itself behind but a smoky red cloud of dust.

END